"You're af...
your ow... ...ons!"

Logan was frowning as he went on, "You're not frightened of me. Are you ashamed to respond?"

"Will you please just go, Logan? It's been a long day," said Raina flatly, "and I want you out."

"No. You want me, period, and you won't admit it! Raina, how long can you keep your feelings in cold storage?"

Raina snapped, "That's my own business. I've been offered your kind of service before!"

"What do you mean?" His eyes blazed questioningly.

She took a deep breath. "You're not the first man to make a pass at me since Perry died. You were his friend, and I thought you were different. I was wrong. I'm a widow and fair game, so join the queue, Logan. But the answer is still no. Do I make myself clear?"

DAPHNE CLAIR

dark remembrance

Harlequin Books

TORONTO • LONDON • LOS ANGELES • AMSTERDAM
SYDNEY • HAMBURG • PARIS • STOCKHOLM • ATHENS • TOKYO

Harlequin Presents edition published October 1981
ISBN 0-373-10458-8

Original hardcover edition published in 1981
by Mills & Boon Limited

CHAPTER ONE

RAINA closed the door of her son's bedroom behind her and slumped against it with weariness. Danny was just getting over a bout of 'flu which had made him unusually fractious, and at less than four he was too young to understand that his constant demands were wearing to his mother's nerves.

She went into the kitchen to make herself a cup of coffee, but had just plugged in the electric jug and taken a cup from the cupboard when the front doorbell pealed.

At this hour! she thought, annoyed at whoever it was, and tensed for the sound of Danny, in case it should have disturbed the sleep into which he had only fallen five minutes ago.

Of course, it wasn't so late—only eight-thirty by the clock as she glanced at it on her way to the short passageway and the door. But when she saw the tall man standing on the little porch, raindrops sprinkling his dark hair and shining on the shoulders of his leather jacket, she greeted him curtly, making his black brows lift in slightly amused interrogation as he stepped into the house.

Raina automatically moved back, allowing him to close the door himself. She always had the impression that Logan Thorne was too big for this house, that she needed to keep out of his way, give him room.

'How are you?' he asked, and she looked away as she said, 'Fine.' The harsh light she had switched on in the hallway accentuated the tired blue shadows beneath her eyes and the hollow look of her cheeks, and she knew that Logan's penetrating ice-blue gaze never missed a thing.

He followed her into the comfortable lounge at the front of the house, and she switched on a standard lamp because the muted light might conceal some of the evidence of her worn-out state.

She said, 'Sit down, Logan,' but he ignored the cushioned blue velvet armchairs and the long matching sofa, and instead took her arm in a firm grasp and turned her towards the lamp, taking her chin in cool fingers to tilt her face so that he could look at it.

She jerked away from his hold, and he let her go. He had seen enough, anyway.

'What have you been doing to yourself?' he asked.

'Nothing!' she snapped. 'I'm a little tired because Danny's been sick.'

'You look awful,' he said with brutal candour, and she gave him a sour smile and said, 'Thanks!'

'Sorry,' he replied, 'but it's true. What's the matter with Dan?'

He never called Daniel *Danny*; it was one of the things about Logan that irritated her.

She said, 'Just a 'flu bug. He had it rather badly.'

'Have you had it, too?' he asked, still not taking a chair.

Raina sat down on the sofa and said, 'Only a touch. I'm over it now.'

Logan thrust back his damp hair from his tanned forehead and looked at her with exasperated derision in his eyes. 'You don't look it, to me. Did you get the doctor?'

'*Yes*,' she said tightly, and tried to hide her anger. 'Would you like some coffee?'

'No. What's the matter now?'

'There isn't anything the matter.'

'Oh, come *on*, Raina! I know I'm not your favourite person, but you don't look daggers at me for nothing!'

'All right,' she said, her green eyes flashing. 'If you must know, I resent the implication that I might not have looked after Danny properly. *Of course* I got the doctor! What did you *think*——?'

'Now, hold on there!' Logan said forcefully, cutting her short. 'I wasn't implying anything of the sort.'

'Weren't you? It certainly sounded like——'

'*No!*' he almost shouted. Then he made a visible effort to control his temper and said more quietly, 'I know damned well you'll get a doctor for Dan any time he seems in need of one. I was worried about whether you'd have the same care for yourself.'

Raina raised her eyes to his face, saw it looking grim and dark and uncompromising. From her angle of vision the stubborn jut of his jaw was accentuated, the mouth above it firmly masculine with a hint of sensuality in the slight fullness of his lower lip, his nose straight, the nostrils a little pinched with controlled anger, and the brows drawn together over those cold blue eyes.

A hint of colour rose in her cheeks, and her pale lips trembled. 'I'm sorry,' she said. She pressed her lips together hard and said, not looking at him, 'For heaven's sake, sit down, Logan!'

She had thought he would take one of the armchairs, and was dismayed when instead he came and sat beside her, half turning to face her, with his arm resting on the back of the sofa.

He was too close, like that, making her uneasy, and she felt her nerves tense. His knuckles brushed briefly, very lightly, against her cheek, and he said, 'It's been rough, has it? I'm sorry I wasn't here.'

She moved her head, slightly but definitely, away from his touch, and saw the knuckles go white as his hand tightened. 'I managed,' she said, shrugging. 'We didn't need you. Really, you've no need to take your—responsibility—for us as heavily as you do. I'm sure Perry didn't intend——'

'Perry made his intentions perfectly clear,' said Logan. 'I don't find it so onerous, you know.'

She looked at him, trying to gauge the meaning of the slight, almost cynical and definitely unamused smile on his lips. 'I think you do,' she contradicted him.

His mouth twisted rather oddly. 'Not in the way you mean,' he answered. 'Anyway, Perry would have done the same for me.'

'But you're not married.'

'That's right. Perry was the lucky one, wasn't he?'

She didn't know about that. Perhaps Logan was right, in a way. Perry had been happy in the few brief years they had been married, adoring Raina and taking a touching pride in his infant son. But he had crashed the light plane he had been flying a year ago, and died some days later in hospital, of multiple injuries that would have crippled him if he had lived.

'He would never have stood life in a wheelchair, you know,' Logan said quietly, as though he had followed her thoughts.

No, he wouldn't have. It would have been a living death for him, for Perry had always loved movement, adventure, speed, risk. He had been stunting with the plane when it crashed, trying to fly under power lines, a trick he had performed without harm before, but which this time proved fatal.

Raina remembered that Logan, at the time, had been more furious than sympathetic, calling Perry a bloody fool and worse, and rhetorically asking what the hell he had thought he was playing at, showing off in a way that was stupid as well as dangerous and illegal.

They had been waiting, he and Raina, at a room in the hospital by then, after the nightmare of helplessly watching the crash, and getting Perry's broken body out of the wreckage and into the ambulance. And when Logan stopped cursing suddenly and said, 'God, Raina! I'm sorry!' she had looked at the anguish in his eyes and the tightly clamped mouth showing white at the edges. She knew that he was suffering, too, and said with a rare surge of understanding, 'It's all right, Logan. I know how you feel.'

And he looked at her across the width of the tiny room and said, simply, 'Yes.'

It was the only time she had seen Logan close to losing control over his emotions, the only time she had felt really close to him. He and Perry had been best friends ever since childhood, when they had been brought up in the same children's home, Logan a true orphan since babyhood, and Perry the product of a broken marriage. Raina had known when she agreed to marry Perry Kimball that she was going to have to accept Logan into her life, as Perry's closest friend. They were then partners in a company that was just getting off the ground, repairing, maintaining and later manufacturing aircraft for local and overseas markets. It hadn't taken Raina long to discover that Perry still harboured the remains of an acute case of hero-worship for Logan Thorne, since the days when the slightly older and bigger boy had shielded a younger, less aggressive Perry from the playground bullies and earned his undying gratitude.

When they became engaged, Logan was in Australia on a trip connected with the setting up of the manufacturing, under licence, of their first fully built airplane, and Perry insisted that the wedding couldn't take place until he returned.

There was no other reason to wait. They were madly in love, Perry had no contact with his parents and Raina's mother had died two years before. Her parents' marriage had faltered and died when she was scarcely five years old, and her father had married again and gone to the South Island and produced three more children. Gradually his interest in her had waned, and she had not heard from him in years. Neither Raina nor Perry had any other family; it was one of the things that had drawn them together, and one of the things they were determined to avoid in their own lives. Their marriage would last, their children would be loved, and provided with brothers and sisters, and given a warm, secure home life just as long as they needed it.

They had started well, but the accident had cruelly cut short all their lovely plans. Sometimes Raina found herself fighting down an angry bitterness, because Perry had had so much to live for, and he had thrown it away so carelessly in a moment for the sake of a piece of childish derring-do.

The coroner had had some sharp words to say about people who took unnecessary risks in light aircraft, adding that at least this particular pilot had not endangered the lives of any passengers, but had been flying alone. And for a moment, sitting in the stark room with Logan beside her, Raina had closed her eyes and wished passionately that she *had* been with Perry, that he had taken her with him when he died.

And Logan had closed his strong fingers over her clenched hands in her lap, and held them until it was all over. It had helped to steady her, and she had begun to think quite deliberately about Danny, two years old and needing his remaining parent, at least, to think of him and care for him, and make up for the loss of his father. She wouldn't let him down, she vowed. She would be everything to him, mother, father, family—he shouldn't be allowed to suffer for this.

She had to be grateful to Logan. He had been a tower of strength in the dark days after the funeral, and she knew that he was hiding a deep and genuine grief of his own, while he gave his time and energy unstintingly to helping her, taking as many of the necessary tasks from her as he could. When she tried to express her gratitude, he said, 'I promised Perry I'd look after you and Dan, Raina. Don't think about it.'

But she had thought about it, and more as the initial shock and grief wore off a little, and she began to re-assert her independence. Raina had never leaned on anyone in her life, and even though for a short time it had been a blessed relief to let Logan take over and do things for her, it wasn't long before she was assuring him she could manage on her own, thanks; his assistance had been welcome but was no longer needed.

He had looked at her with a grim little smile, and said, 'Okay, I get the message, but I'll still keep an eye on you and young Dan. Perry wanted it. And you know that you can call on me at any time.'

'Yes. Thank you. I don't think that Perry intended his family to be an albatross about your neck for the rest of your life, Logan.'

He laughed, the first time she had seen him laugh, except for Danny's benefit, since the funeral. Then he looked at her with a disturbing awareness in his eyes and said quietly, 'Some albatross!'

Raina turned away sharply, rejecting that look. She didn't want any man's eyes on her like that, reminding her of the smooth, lovely planes of her face, the slight, delicate arching of her brows over clear green eyes, a firmly pretty mouth, shining, thick dark brown hair swinging on to her shoulders, and a figure that Perry used to describe as absolutely perfect. Not any man's eyes—but especially not Logan Thorne's.

He had been best man at their wedding, and she had met him for the first time at the rehearsal in the church the night before. It wasn't going to be a big wedding, but Perry and Raina wanted it to be a nice one, with flowers and a bridesmaid and music to dress up the simple church ceremony—something to describe to their children in future years.

Logan was a surprise—she had formed a picture of him in her mind and expected a big, goodhumoured man, something like a slightly fierce, overgrown teddy bear. When she arrived at the church and Perry introduced Logan, she had been momentarily stunned. This was no teddy bear. This was a tiger. He was big all right—big and powerful and dangerous. She wasn't even sure how she knew that, but there was something about him that spelled it out—watch out, don't get in my way.

She had been wryly pleased that Perry hadn't waited for Logan's approval before asking her to marry him, and when she met Logan her first thought was that she was glad he had been away in Australia at the time—because if he hadn't liked her, he would have broken up the affair in no time. She just knew in her bones that he would have, somehow, and without compunction. He gave her a long, assessing look as she held out her hand, and his fingers closed about hers strongly, holding them while his blue eyes scanned her face. Then his mouth smiled, but not his eyes, and he nodded as though approving of her. 'I've already congratulated Perry,' he drawled. 'I do it again!'

His voice said he liked her looks, but she wasn't flattered, because his eyes were wondering if she could live up to her looks, and he didn't mind a bit that she knew it.

She had been prepared to like Logan Thorne, for Perry's sake. If he had been the kind of man she had expected, she might have found an opportunity to assure him that she would make his friend a good wife, that they loved each other very much, and their marriage was going to be a wonderful one.

Instead, she felt defensive, and when he touched her hand her fingers stiffened in his, because she felt in a strange way that he had captured her, that his warm hard grasp was meant to hold her while he inspected her and decided if she was good enough for Perry.

When he let her go, her fingers tingled with the warmth he had transferred to them. She flexed them surreptitiously, but he noticed and raised a mocking dark eyebrow, querying her action. He knew his grasp had been firm but not hard. She felt a quick flash of antagonism, and met his eyes with a cool and haughty look. *I don't like you*, she thought. *But you're Perry's friend, and I can never let him guess.*

Perry never had guessed, because both Raina and Logan had taken pains to keep him happy. Perry had a natural, lighthearted innocence, and a gift for getting on with people. It was inconceivable to Perry that the two people he loved most would fail to like each other, and he simply assumed from the start that naturally Raina and Logan would be friends.

After they signed the register on their wedding day, he encouraged Logan to claim the privilege of kissing the bride, and Raina stood rigid within the circle of her new husband's arm while Logan tipped her chin with a hard brown hand, and looked down for a blinding instant, his eyes now a fiery blue, as they met the mute rejection in hers. Then he bent his head with tantalising slowness and pressed his cool lips briefly and firmly against hers.

It was several moments before Raina could unclench her teeth and smile again at Perry, and in her mind there was one fierce, emphatic resolve: *I will never let him touch me again.*

She often wished she had never had to see him again, but because of Perry that was impossible. The two men were not only business partners, but close friends. When Perry told Raina that Logan had refused several invitations to visit them after they settled into their new home, on the grounds that the newlyweds could hardly want a third party intruding on their happiness, she knew what he wanted. The next day she phoned Logan with an invitation, and told him Perry would be hurt if he didn't accept. From then on, he was a frequent visitor. He was Perry's obvious choice for godfather when Daniel was christened, and Raina smiled in spite of a sinking heart and asked the girl who had been her bridesmaid to act as godmother.

Carol had been delighted, not so much at the invitation to sponsor Daniel as the opportunity to be coupled with Logan again. After the wedding he had taken Carol out on the town, and given her, she said, a fabulous time, but although she had met him again several times at Raina's and Perry's house, the invitation had never been repeated.

Nor was it on the occasion of Daniel's christening, although Logan remembered Carol and was casually pleasant to her.

'I spent a fortune on this outfit!' she wailed to Raina as they tucked the baby into his cot after Logan had taken his leave. 'And he scarcely looked at me!'

It wasn't true, Raina knew—he had actually spent quite a lot of time talking to Carol, who had waylaid him at every not too obvious opportunity. But he had not asked her to go out with him. Now she was peering

anxiously into the mirror on the bedroom wall, surveying her pretty blonde curls and her equally pretty face,
the nicely lipsticked mouth now downturned with dis-
appointment, but still tempting enough, Raina would
have thought, for any man but Logan Thorne. 'What's
the matter with me?' Carol asked glumly. 'Doesn't he
like blondes?'

Not like you, Raina knew with absolute certainty. He
liked blondes, all right, and brunettes and all shades in
between, as far as she could tell. He often had a girl in
tow; there was never any problem about making up a
foursome for an outing with Logan and the girl of the
moment. But Carol was soft and sweet and kindhearted,
of average intelligence and possessed of a touching
loyalty to her friends; Raina was very fond of her, and
thought that she was far too good for Logan. She said
so, adding, 'I don't know why you should want him,
anyway. What's so attractive about Logan?'

Carol turned an astonished gaze on her and said, 'You
mean you don't *know*?'

'He's not all that good-looking,' said Raina, giving
the blanket a last firm tuck and leaving her sleepy son's
side. 'Is he?'

'Not——? Well, of course he is—in a sort of rugged
way—he sends shivers up my spine.'

'I'm not surprised,' Raina said grimly. 'It's those cold
blue eyes.'

'I thought he was a friend of yours!' Carol said.

'He's a friend of Perry's. Believe me, Carol, he isn't
your sort. His girl-friends are the hard cold type, like
him. Clever and calculating and out for number one.
You're not like that—you'd get hurt.'

She could see that Carol didn't believe her, but she
wasn't going to get anywhere with Logan because he
simply wasn't interested. Shortly after that Carol went

overseas for a working holiday. She met an Englishman, married him, and never came back to New Zealand. She still corresponded with Raina, and sent photographs of herself and her husband, who looked tall and dark and had a long, intelligent face and kindly. dark eyes. Carol appeared to be blissfully happy.

'*Raina!*' said Logan, his voice sharp. 'It's all over now. Try not to think about it.'

She realised that she had been ignoring Logan, while memories of the past flooded her tired mind, and she said automatically, 'I'm sorry, Logan. What were you saying?'

'Nothing. I shouldn't have mentioned Perry. It's you that matters now. How long since you ate a decent meal?'

'I'm all right. I just need some sleep.'

'How long?' he repeated, and she sighed. Logan wouldn't give up, she knew.

'I don't know,' she said. 'I haven't been hungry—lunch, I think.'

'What was it? Sardines on toast?'

'Scrambled egg,' she said. 'I'm not stupid—I have to have energy to look after Danny.'

'Lunch,' he repeated sarcastically. 'And now it's nearly nine. Stay there and I'll get you something.'

She protested, but he was adamant, pushing her back on the sofa when she made to rise, saying, 'I know my way round your kitchen. Now *sit!*'

As though I was a dog! she thought resentfully. But she was too tired even to feel resentment for long, and when he brought in a tray with thick tinned soup steaming in a bowl and a plate of toasted ham sandwiches, she was grudgingly grateful.

He took one sandwich himself, then sat watching her

eat, and when she asked, 'When did *you* last eat?' he grinned and said, 'A couple of hours ago, on the plane.'

She looked up then, startled, and for the first time realised that she wasn't the only one who was tired. His tan hid any paleness, but there were lines of strain about his eyes, and a couple of times he had put a hand to the back of his neck as if easing away stiffness.

'You came straight here?' she said.

He merely nodded, as though there was nothing to be added.

She asked, 'How was the trip?'

'Successful. I spoke to the designers about the problems we've been having in the construction of the latest model, and I think we've ironed it out. And the Australian branch is coming along nicely.'

He went into some more technical detail and Raina listened carefully. He always told her what was going on in the firm, she still drew an income from it—Perry's share, although Perry had more than earned it, and Logan had firmly vetoed any suggestion that Raina might shoulder some of the work, at least until Danny went to school. Not that she could have done Perry's job. He was a genius with engines, had an instinct for them, Logan had once said. Raina had sometimes wondered unfairly if it was this, rather than their friendship which had prompted Logan to suggest a partnership. Only Logan's grief at Perry's death had finally dispelled that suspicion.

But she might have made herself useful about the office or on the non-technical staff, somewhere. She was a quick learner and not unintelligent—moreover, she held a private pilot's licence herself.

But Logan had refused to even discuss the possibility of a job for her until Danny was five—and as far as the company was concerned, what Logan said was law.

Even when Perry was alive, he had left decisions to Logan, saying that Logan was the brains of the company, and he himself the brawn. It always made people laugh, because although Perry was fit and wiry, he had an almost faun-like quality of masculine grace, nothing brawny about him, and certainly he hadn't been stupid. But where his instinct was for engines and what made them tick—or not—Logan undoubtedly had an instinct for the financial side of the company's business. He knew when to expand, when to try a new venture, when to take a risk, and he had never been wrong yet. The company had gone from strength to strength under his direction.

Not that Logan was ignorant of the technical side. He did a lot of test flying and delivery flights himself, and could take an engine apart and put it together, but he had acknowledged Perry's special gift, and always deferred to his opinion in that area.

Logan had stopped talking, and was taking her plate from her. 'I'll make you some coffee,' he said, and she asked with automatic politeness, 'Will you join me?'

The corners of his mouth lifted a little. 'Sure. Thanks.'

When he came back, she said, 'Thank *you*, Logan. You're very good to us.'

'Aren't I?' he said sardonically. 'A pity you resent it so much.'

She took the cup he handed her, sipped the coffee he had made just as she preferred it, strong, sugarless, but with a smidgeon of cream stirred into it. 'Why do you say that?' she asked.

'It's true.' He sat beside her again, putting his own cup of straight black coffee on a side table within easy reach. He lounged in the corner of the sofa, his arm again resting on the back, his eyes hard.

To avoid them, she sipped at her coffee again, and kept her own eyes down as she lowered her cup. 'I'm sorry, if I seem ungrateful,' she said carefully. 'I do happen to be an independent sort of person, I suppose.'

'It isn't that,' he said, with a hint of impatience. 'And you know I don't want gratitude!'

'Then what do you want?' Raina asked.

For a moment he was silent. Then he said softly, 'Now there's a question.'

She looked up then, and found his eyes surveying her with a strange, speculative look. She shifted uneasily, aware that the silence was lengthening, and that there was something in the quality of his gaze that was definitely disturbing. She wanted to break the moment, dispel the sudden tension. Raising her brows delicately, she said, 'You're not making a pass at me, are you, Logan?'

He kept looking at her for a moment or two before he replied, apparently weighing his answer. Then he said, 'Have I ever made a pass at you, Raina?'

She hesitated before saying, 'No.'

'Have you ever wanted me to?'

Her eyes widening with anger, she said, *No!*

She turned her head sharply away from him, but he moved his hand and caught at her chin, bringing her to face him again. His eyes had changed to a piercing scrutiny. 'How long do you expect this beautiful friendship of ours to last, Raina?' he asked.

'You're Perry's friend,' she said. 'Not mine.'

She put up a hand to push at his wrist, and he let go her chin and captured her fingers in his. 'Perry's been dead over a year, now,' he reminded her. 'But you and I still see each other pretty frequently.'

'Because of your sense of obligation,' she said swiftly.

His fingers tightened on her hand and she looked

down and said, 'You're hurting me.'

He released her at once. 'A sense of obligation,' he repeated slowly. 'You think that's my only reason for looking out for you—and Dan?'

'I know you're fond of Danny,' she admitted.

With a hint of sarcasm, he said, 'You do. And that leaves out you, doesn't it? Tell me how I feel about *you*, why don't you?'

She stood up to put her cup on a table, although there was still some coffee in it. 'I wouldn't know,' she said indifferently. She straightened to face him, and found him on his feet, too, watching her with an oddly frustrated frown between his brows.

'Then maybe it's time you did!' he said, and suddenly came close, reaching for her.

She had no chance to move away as his hands clamped on her waist, pulling her against him. She pushed at his upper arms, making no impression at all, and then his mouth came down on hers in a searching, hard kiss, his arms sliding further about her to hold her to the length of his strong masculine body.

Her first reaction was shock, pure and simple. The touch of his mouth was strange and almost brutal, totally without the tenderness that had always been present in Perry's kisses. For a moment she stopped trying to push him away, her mind spinning in confusion. His body heat was penetrating through her clothes, and a slow warmth of her own began to flow through her veins. His mouth began to move with deliberate seductiveness on hers, and she experienced a sudden urgent desire to respond. Momentarily she opened her lips to his, but then she realised fully what was happening to her, and wrenched her mouth away, her choked voice crying, *'No!'*

His hand pushed into her hair, and he found her

mouth again, but now she was fighting him, and when he gave up and let her go, she swung her hand back and slapped him hard.

His face was flushed under the tan, and for a moment her fingermarks showed white on his cheek. His eyes glittered furiously for an instant, then he stepped back and laughed.

'Spitfire!' he said. 'Is that supposed to demonstrate how you feel about *me*?'

'That's about it!' she snapped, shaking with anger. 'Don't you ever touch me again! I can't *stand* you! I never could. Now, will you please get out?'

He looked at her, his mouth a wry line. 'What do you plan to do? Stay loyal to Perry's memory for the rest of your life? You're only twenty-four and you're not frigid. You've had a year of long cold nights alone. It can't go on for ever.'

'I said, *get out*!'

'You've got to start living again some time, Raina——'

'*Not* with you!' she said. 'Never with *you*!'

Logan's mouth tightened. 'With no one else. Perry's dead, Raina. You don't have to fight it any more.'

Before she could even absorb all the implications of that, he had left, his long strides carrying him to the door in seconds, only the echoing slam of the door, and her turbulent thoughts, left behind him.

CHAPTER TWO

'WAIKATO weather,' Raina murmured resignedly as she pulled back the curtains of her bedroom and found a grey, clinging damp fog hanging over the garden. She shivered, and pulled her warm yellow dressing gown tighter about her. Yellow wasn't a colour she wore much, but Danny had persuaded her to buy this, saying it looked 'sunshiny', and he always called it her sunshine gown. There hadn't been much sunshine in their lives then, with Perry's death only beginning to fade from immediate horror into remembered misery, and she had put aside the blue and the purple dressing gowns the saleswoman had been showing her, and immediately decided on the yellow for Danny's sake.

Well, it didn't look as though there would be much sunshine today. This kind of dull fog in the morning often hung about until noon. A frost was preferable, because there was an even chance it would be followed by a clear, cloudless sunny day. She had hoped that she might be able to get Danny up today, and into one of the cushioned loungers on the north-facing porch which caught the winter sun.

He hadn't stirred yet, and he had slept through the night for the first time since he had become sick. Raina hadn't slept nearly so well. She told herself it was because she had been alert for a sound from Danny, in case she was needed. But the thoughts that had kept her brain churning had not all been of Danny. Her mind, her body, had insisted on reliving over and over again the few moments when Logan Thorne had suddenly, unexpectedly, taken her in his arms and kissed her—

22

and brought her to an equally sudden and unexpected pitch of desire.

She didn't think that he had known it. Fervently, she hoped he hadn't. She had only allowed herself one moment of weakness before sanity returned and she had pushed him away. And that was all it was, she told herself—a moment of weakness, a purely physical reaction to being held and kissed by a man, after a whole year without any sexual contact. She was a normal healthy woman, and since the first shock of grief had subsided, she had often ached with longing for the physical closeness of her husband. But Perry wasn't there any more. And although her body would have accepted a substitute, her mind vetoed that. Logan—any man—might be able to stir her senses, fulfil a primeval biological need. But no man could take Perry's place in her heart, and certainly not Logan Thorne. Least of all Logan Thorne.

She turned away from the depressing sight of the fog outside, and picked up a hairbrush, stroking it vigorously over her hair. Then she quietly went into the kitchen and made herself some toast and tea.

She was putting her dishes into the stainless steel sink, when Danny's plaintive voice called her. When she went in to him, he was sitting up in the bed, his fine brown hair falling over his darker brown eyes. His baby features were scarcely formed, and yet there were times when his likeness to his father made her eyes sting with suppressed tears.

'I'm hungry!' he announced truculently.

Raina laughed and sat down on the edge of the bed to push back his hair with her fingers and drop a light kiss on his smooth forehead. 'Are you, darling? Well, that's good. Would you like to put on your dressing gown and slippers, and get up for breakfast?'

He considered that, then said definitely, 'Yes!'

'Good. Here you are, then.' She helped him, and sent him off to the bathroom while she prepared cornflakes and fruit in the kitchen, humming softly to herself, because Danny hadn't been hungry for days, and she was sure now he was really on the mend.

About lunchtime, the fog lifted, and although there was a nippy breeze in the air, Raina decided to do some gardening while Danny had an afternoon nap. At least it would get her outside into the fresh air. She changed into faded jeans and an old jersey, tied back her hair with a scarf, and descended on the roses, which were overdue for pruning. The roses had come with the house, a bed of spectacular blooms from deep blood red to creamy gold and pure virginal white. The previous owner had obviously lavished every care on them, and Raina had felt honour bound to do her best to continue it.

There were daffodils beginning to show yellow petals, and snowdrops nodding prettily around the base of the kowhai in one corner of the garden. Signs of spring, Raina thought, and that was nice. Winter had seemed overlong this year. The Waikato in winter could be depressing, but it was the most lush grassland in the country, famous for its dairy herds, and beautiful in the spring, when the grass was burgeoning in emerald green, the fruit trees bursting out in white and pink frilly blossom, the willows and the poplars clothing their winter-bare branches in new yellow-green leaf, and the lambs and calves and foals following at their mothers' heels in the paddocks.

The roses looked chastened after their pruning, but in summer the house would be filled with bowls of them, scented with their voluptuous fragrance. Perry had loved them, although he had laughed at her efforts to learn how to care for the bushes, saying they would still flower if they were left alone to grow as they wanted.

Raina left the prunings in a heap by the roses, to be gathered up later, and pulled some weeds from some of the other flower beds. By the time she finished, the gardening gloves she wore were caked with dirt, and her jeans were filthy. Wisps of hair escaped the scarf, and she pushed them out of her eyes impatiently as she massaged an aching back and went to collect the wheelbarrow to carry the rose prunings to the rubbish heap at the back of the house.

She scooped up handfuls of the rose cuttings, some with wicked-looking thorns on them, and dropped them into the barrow, so intent that she must have missed the sound of the car. When she heard Logan's voice behind her, she jumped and straitened suddenly, a convulsive movement of her hands bringing a sharp thorn in contact with one exposed wrist.

Her exclamation was half surprise and half pain, and she dropped the bundle of clippings into the barrow and automatically lifted her wrist to find the source of the sharp ache just above the cuff of her glove.

Logan said, 'Let me see!' and took her hand, stripping off the glove and flinging it to the ground as he drew in a sharp breath at the sight of the great curved thorn embedded in the soft inner flesh of her wrist. 'Keep still,' he said, and grasped the protruding base, gently easing it out with the fine point still intact.

Raina bit her lip and didn't move, but when the blood welled, and Logan bent and put his mouth to the spot, she snatched her hand away.

He looked at her with a curiously opaque gaze, and said, 'You'll need a dressing on that. How did you come to do it?'

'You startled me,' she said.

His voice was curt when he said, 'Sorry. Come on, you'd better get inside and I'll see to that.'

She pulled off her other glove, bending to pick up the first one and drop them both on the handle of the wheelbarrow. 'I can do it,' she said. She was suddenly annoyingly conscious of her scruffy appearance, the dirty gardening clothes, her dishevelled hair, and no doubt streaks of dirt where she had pushed windblown strands from her eyes.

Logan opened the back door as she kicked off her gumboots. 'I'm sure you can,' he was saying. 'But it's your right hand and it'll be easier if you have help.'

Raina went to the bathroom, and he followed, taking the first aid box from her as she removed it from the cupboard, and waiting with disinfectant and a plaster ready as she washed the blood away under the tap.

He handed her a piece of cotton wool, and watched her dry her wrist and resignedly hold it out to him for his ministrations. He dabbed on some disinfectant and placed the plaster firmly, saying as he did so, 'Is it everyone, or just me?'

'What are you talking about?' she asked.

'All this stubborn independence of yours,' he said, tossing the used cotton wool into the toilet bowl and snapping shut the first aid box. 'Is it just me you hate accepting help from, or do you reject it from everyone?'

'I don't reject it,' she answered. 'I've told you before, I'm grateful for what you've done for Danny and me——'

He made an impatient exclamation, and she said, 'Why don't you wait in the lounge? I'd like to wash and change, if you don't mind.'

He turned and went without a word, and she closed the door after him and ran warm water into the basin.

When she joined him ten minutes later, she had changed into a soft cream woollen dress and combed out her hair into a shining bell that just brushed her shoulders. Spike-heeled shoes gave her height, although she had to look up a little to meet Logan's eyes, and pink lipstick emphasised the firm fullness of her mouth.

Logan hadn't sat down, but turned from staring out at the garden as she came into the room. He said, 'You've been doing too much. If you'd told me the roses needed pruning——'

'You'd have sent someone to do it,' she said. 'I know. And I look terrible. You said so last night.'

'No, you don't,' he said, as though he resented it. 'You look beautiful and you know it.'

Her heart did something odd, and she said quickly, 'Would you like a drink?'

'No, thanks.' He had hesitated before he answered, not because he was thinking about it, she knew, but because he wanted to underline the fact that he was allowing her to change the subject.

'I like gardening,' she said. 'I've scarcely been out of the house since Danny's been sick.'

'How is he?'

'Better. He's asleep, now.'

'Let me take you out to dinner tonight.'

'No, I don't want to leave him. And I'm tired, as you've noticed.'

'You need to get out. Mrs Crimmins would look after Dan.'

'No.'

They were both still standing, facing each other. Logan held her eyes with his and said quietly, 'You'd have said no, anyway, wouldn't you? Even if Dan was bursting with health and you weren't exhausted with looking after him.'

'If you're staying, you'd better sit down,' she said, turning away from him.

'I've had more gracious invitations.'

'I'm sorry.' She stood by a chair, her hand on the back of it, smoothing the blue velvet absently with her fingertips. 'Can't I get you a cup of tea or something?'

'Okay, if you'll make yourself one,' he said. 'I won't offer to help.'

Because she would refuse was the unspoken implication. Raina noted the unusually bitter note in his voice, and felt a twinge of compunction.

She had made cheese scones for lunch, because Danny had asked for them. There were several left over, and she buttered them and put them on a plate to add to the tray with the two cups of tea.

When she came to the door of the lounge, Logan was sitting in a chair with his head against the back of it, his strong profile looking oddly bleak as he stared at a spot on the ceiling. He turned his head to look at her as she came into the room, and for a moment the bleakness remained, until he smiled faintly and said, 'That looks terrific.'

He had demolished a scone and was reaching for another when she asked, 'Haven't you had any lunch?'

'No. I wanted to get away early——'

'To see me?'

His eyes mocked her surprise. 'That's right. About last night—Raina, I——'

'If you want to apologise,' she said swiftly, 'don't bother. Let's just forget it, shall we?'

She was looking down at her cup, her body tense. She couldn't see his expression.

After a moment he said, 'No, I wasn't going to apologise.'

She glanced up and saw an odd kind of anger in his

eyes as they rested on her. 'Well, I don't see any need to discuss it, then,' she said crisply. 'I'm sure it won't happen again.'

'Are you?' he said, deliberately. 'I'm not.'

Raina drew in her breath, and met his eyes again with an effort. 'If it does,' she said very clearly, 'then I'm afraid I shall have to ask you never to visit my home again.'

His mouth thinned, and the anger in his eyes flamed dangerously. Raina's nerves tautened.

Then they were interrupted by Danny, who erupted into the room, flinging himself at Logan and saying indignantly, 'Uncle Logan *got* to visit us, Mummy! Why don't he never visit us again?'

Raina started to say, 'You don't understand, Danny,' but Logan's voice cut across hers as he pulled the child on to his knee and said, 'It's all right, Dan. Mummy didn't mean it.'

His eyes met hers in challenge over the top of the tousled little head. Raina sat in frustrated silence, as Danny sent her a puzzled, worried look. 'Don't mean it, Mummy?' he asked hopefully.

She hesitated, and Logan said, 'Of course not. She was just playing a game.'

'What game?' Danny asked, turning to him with rounded eyes.

'A grown-up game,' Logan explained steadily, his eyes fleetingly clashing with Raina's again.

'Play a game with *me*, Uncle Logan!' Danny demanded, apparently satisfied with the explanation.

'Okay, sport. But let me finish my tea first.'

'I got to get it,' Danny announced, and wriggled off his perch to run back to his room.

Raina looked away from the amused knowledge in Logan's eyes. He knew she wouldn't ban him from seeing Danny. The boy was very attached to his 'Uncle' Logan, the only stable masculine influence in his life since Perry had died, and therefore of great importance to him.

She got up, holding her empty cup, and without speaking to him again, took his and placed them both on the tray.

'I'll take it,' he said, and she stepped back as he rose from the chair to carry the tray back into the kitchen. She followed, and began filling the sink as he put down the tray. 'Will you stay for dinner?' she asked stiffly.

'Is that an olive branch?'

'It would be good for Danny,' she said coolly. 'He still misses his father.'

'Do *you* still miss Perry?'

Anger exploded in her. She turned on him and snapped, her voice high and hard, 'What the hell do you *think*?'

'Yes,' he said in clipped tones. 'I shouldn't have asked.'

Raina swung round and turned off the taps, then tipped the cups and saucers into the warm water, squirting in some detergent with a vigour that made too many suds. Her mouth was tight, and her hands shook.

Logan moved to stand behind her, his hands shaping her shoulders, but she went rigid and he dropped them. 'I didn't quite mean it like that,' he said, his voice sounding a little roughened. 'I know you miss him, but there must be a point where you come to terms with having lost him. *Your* life hasn't ended.'

She heard her son's voice calling him, and said, 'Danny wants you.'

Logan raised his voice and called back, 'Coming!' Then he said softly, 'Raina, you can't run away from it forever.'

Danny called again, then appeared in the kitchen doorway clutching a snakes and ladders board and a cup of dice. Logan said, 'Yes, Dan, I'm coming.' As he turned to join the boy he said to Raina, 'I'll stay to dinner.'

Logan washed up after their meal, while Raina put Danny to bed. She spun the process out, letting Danny play in the bath, and choosing a long story to read to him from his favourite book of fairy tales. Logan appeared in the doorway as she reached the happy-ever-after ending. She tried to ignore him as she kissed Danny's cheek and received a hug and kiss in return, but Danny wanted to give him a goodnight kiss, too. Logan returned it and ruffled the child's hair with a large hand as Danny wriggled down under the blankets again. 'Have a good sleep,' said Logan. 'You need it, and so does your mother.'

Danny smiled in a puzzled way, and asked, 'Why's Mummy need it?'

'Because she's tired herself out, looking after you, sport. So try not to bother her tonight unless you really need to, okay?'

'Okay.' The boy's glance went past Logan to Raina, hovering in the doorway. 'You better go to bed, too, Mummy.'

'Yes, darling. I will, soon,' she promised.

She switched off the light as Logan passed her, and followed him back to the lounge. There were two steaming cups of coffee on the low table before the sofa, and he pushed her gently into sitting down, and handed her a cup before lowering himself beside her.

'You had no reason to tell Danny that,' she said. 'Now he'll worry about me, and might be frightened to call if he does need me.'

'I had every reason,' he retorted. 'It won't hurt him to learn a bit of consideration.'

'He's only three!'

'I know how old he is.'

'Well, you might remember it! You treat him as though he was at least twice that, sometimes!'

Logan looked at her levelly, and said, 'I treat him like a human being, a young one, but intelligent for all that. He's not a baby, Raina.'

'But he *is*.'

'He's growing out of the baby stage. In a little over a year he'll be at school.' He watched the fleeting expression of anguish that crossed her face, and said, 'Drink your coffee.'

She sipped at it, and he took his and leaned back, drinking the hot brew so quickly she wondered he didn't burn the skin off his tongue.

She was only half finished when he put his empty cup back on the table and said, 'Do you still want a job in the firm when Dan goes to school?'

'I'm drawing an income from it—I want to make some contribution.'

'Perry worked for peanuts those first few years when we were starting up. You're entitled to his share of the profits, now. I've told you that before.'

'*You* worked for peanuts, too.'

'And now I'm reaping the benefits. Would you like a flying job? Deliveries—not testing.'

'*No!*'

Logan raised his dark brows. 'You're very emphatic.'

Raina looked away from him, her hands gripping each other until she deliberately eased her tense fingers. 'Danny has already lost one parent through flying. I couldn't run the risk of it happening again.'

'I wouldn't let you run any risks. I'm not asking you to do trick flying.'

'Are you telling me flying jobs are the only ones available?'

'Heavens, no!' he said impatiently. 'I just thought you'd like something more interesting than sitting behind a desk.'

'Sitting behind a desk is nice and safe,' she said tightly. 'For Danny's sake, I'll stick with that, thanks.'

'You'd do anything for him, wouldn't you?'

She looked at him and saw his eyes were speculative, perhaps a little critical. 'Yes, of course I would,' she said. 'I'm his mother—I'm all he has, now.'

'Don't overdo it, Raina.'

She raised her chin and demanded, 'What do you mean?'

'I mean that you could be—over-protective. And that can't be good for either Daniel or you.'

'I don't think that how I choose to bring up my son is any of your business, Logan.'

He gave her a long, measuring look, and she stared back, refusing to lower her eyes first.

'Whether you like it or not,' he said slowly, 'you and Dan *are* my business. Perry asked me to look out for you both, and I won't welsh on my promise to him. In lots of ways, we were closer than brothers. I can't tell you how to bring up your own son, and I wouldn't try. But I will tell you if I think you're making mistakes. I owe Perry that. I can't force you to agree with me, but I think you've enough intelligence and gumption to at least consider another opinion on its merits. I'm not saying I know better than you, just that sometimes another viewpoint can help. If Perry had lived, you would have discussed Dan's upbringing between the two of you, wouldn't you?'

'Of course, but you're not Perry.'

'That's right, I'm not.' His voice was harsh, suddenly. 'But I'm the boy's godfather, and I'm prepared to take that relationship pretty seriously. You may not like it, but you'll have to accept it.'

'I do accept that. But I won't accept—interference.'

His mouth tightened. 'If that's how you see it, it's too bad,' he shrugged.

'I don't mean to be ungracious,' said Raina. 'I know you mean well——'

'Oh, for God's sake!' he said irritably. 'Spare me that!'

He stood up, and she stood with him, saying, 'You know how grateful I am for all you've done, Logan——'

'Yes, I know! And if you mention it just once more, I'll shake you, Raina, so help me!'

She bit her lip. 'Well, you know that if I could repay you in any way——'

'You mean you'd give anything not to feel in my debt, don't you?' he enquired rather nastily.

His eyes were icy with anger, and she met them with green fire in her own. 'Something like that, yes,' she admitted frankly.

He smiled, without warmth. *'Anything?'* he repeated silkily, and suddenly she recalled last night, and his lips on hers, his hands holding her closely to his hard body. Involuntarily she took a step back from him.

It wasn't far enough. Logan shot out a hand, and hard fingers curved about her nape, pulling her towards him. She met the angry mockery in his eyes and said, 'You wouldn't——'

Still holding her, he drawled, 'No—I wouldn't.'

He let her go suddenly, and she turned away, her heart

pounding with reaction. His voice said tauntingly,
'Disappointed?'

She whirled round, then, her eyes flashing with
temper. '*You'd* be lucky!' she said witheringly, and
Logan laughed.

Her eyes went wary as his hand reached for her again,
but he only caught at her hair, and gave it a hard little
tug as he said, 'I think I've outstayed my welcome.
Goodnight, Raina.'

The following day was cold and cloudy, but Raina
needed to do some shopping, and she asked Mrs
Crimmins, her next-door neighbour, to keep an eye on
Danny for a couple of hours in the afternoon. Mrs
Crimmins was a widow in her sixties, and always seemed
quite willing to babysit, although Raina didn't like to
ask too often.

Their street was a small cul-de-sac, and the other res-
idents were middle-aged couples, the wives going out to
work during the day. Raina knew them all by name, and
they had offered all kinds of help when Perry had died,
but none were really friends. She had made some younger
friends through taking Danny to the local play-centre,
and been invited to the occasional coffee morning, but
other invitations were few since she had lost Perry.
Parties and dinners were for couples, except for the odd
one or two where some unattached male had rather
obviously been invited for her benefit, a gesture which
she appreciated but could have done without. It had
shocked her that not only some of these unattached men
but the husbands of some of her friends had the idea
she would be grateful for a chance to indulge in some
casual sex. After fending off some crude passes, she
ceased attending parties, even when she did get a rare
invitation, and of course in time the invitations dried up.

The town was a country centre, with a large dairy factory serving the farms of the district, several small industries, and a long main street lined with modest shops to sustain its population of less than two thousand. The shopping area had been built on flat land near the river that in the previous century had been used as a supply route, and some of the houses on their neat quarter-acre sections had been built on the surrounding rolling hills. It was an hour's drive from the city of Hamilton, where Logan preferred to live, and less than twenty minutes away from the firm's headquarters, where the planes were assembled and tested.

Perry and Raina had decided to live in Te Ahu because it was so close to his work, and it seemed a good place to bring up a family. There were three smallish primary schools and a large college with a good academic tradition behind it in the town, and all the conveniences of a fair-sized shopping centre, while the countryside was never more than a few minutes away, for as soon as one left the outskirts, the hills expanded into farmland liberally sprinkled with cattle, sheep and horses, neatly divided with post and wire fences and the occasional dark green hedge or row of trees. Here and there a fold in the hills held a pocket of lace-branched ponga ferns, white-blossoming manuka and tall prickly-leaved totara, reminders of the native forests which the pioneers had burned off or cut down to carve out the now tamed and prosperous farmland.

Te Ahu was quiet and clean, friendly and perhaps a little dull. Raina had not noticed the dullness when Perry was alive, she had needed no other stimulation than his vivid, exhilarating personality.

She had thought of moving into Hamilton—Logan had offered to find her a place—but had decided that Perry's death was enough of a bewildering loss for

Danny, without the added strain of losing the home he had always known. She felt he needed as much stability as she could provide, so although the house and the town were full of poignant reminders, she had refused Logan's offer and stayed where she was.

Mrs Crimmins was giving Danny a snack in the kitchen, when Raina returned from her shopping expedition. The little boy looked bright-eyed and had lost the flush of fever which had worried Raina over the past few days. He had also completely recovered his appetite, she noticed, watching him tuck into biscuits and fruit.

'He'll be right now,' Mrs Crimmins assured her comfortably. She had never had children of her own, but she loved them and had fostered a succession of little ones in her younger days. Raina was inclined to listen to her advice when she was moved to give it.

'Have a cup of tea with me, Mrs Crimmins,' she suggested, and the older woman accepted immediately. Raina put on the electric jug and took out cups, pushing aside the two large brown bags of groceries to be put away later.

Over their cups, informally sitting at the kitchen table, they chatted for a while about price rises and the weather, until Danny finished his milk and trotted off to his bedroom to play with his plastic trains which were the passion of the moment. Raina poured herself a second cup of tea, and said, 'Mrs Crimmins, do you think I'm too over-protective with Danny?'

Mrs Crimmins put down her cup, smoothed her full-blown, motherly bosom with one hand to brush away biscuit crumbs, and fixed kind but shrewd brown eyes on Raina's face. 'It would be very easy to be that way,' she said.

'But *am* I?' Raina persisted.

'Maybe. Who suggested that you were?'

'Logan.'

'Ah! I saw he was here, last night. Sorry, dear, I'm not being a nosy neighbour, but I couldn't help noticing his car when I took out the milk bottles.'

'No, of course not,' said Raina. 'You agree with him, don't you?'

'Not exactly. I think you worry too much about Danny, that's for sure. Maybe you can hide that from him. But it won't do *you* any good. You're a good mother, Raina, but you're trying to be two parents, not one. It isn't good for you, and eventually it's going to affect Danny, too. You've been getting thinner lately, and I've seen the shadows round your eyes. Try to relax a bit, there's a good girl.'

'Easier said than done,' Raina said ruefully. 'It's only since Danny has had this wretched 'flu. Now that he's better, I'll be all right.'

'Until he gets chicken-pox, or a tummy bug or mumps,' Mrs Crimmins said. 'What you need is——'

'A tonic?' said Raina, smiling a little wryly. 'Not tranquillisers?'

Mrs Crimmins made a disgusted sound. 'Not those things, no! I'm sure they're very useful for those that really need them, but feeding drugs to young women to keep them going when what they really need is a bit of understanding and someone to help them carry the burden of their families, that's wicked.'

'Well, I'm sure I don't need them,' said Raina. 'I've only one small boy to care for—there's a woman who comes to play-centre who has five, and her husband just walked out on them one day. I haven't much to complain of.'

'Maybe not. But you could do with someone to help ease the burden, all the same. You need a husband.'

Raina blinked, then laughed a little shakily. 'Marry again? I don't think I could. Men like Perry don't grow on trees, you know.'

'It would be a mistake to be looking for another Perry,' Mrs Crimmins said. 'You'd be bound to be disappointed. 'But there are other good men.'

'Maybe. I haven't met them.'

Mrs Crimmins said, 'Isn't Mr Thorne a good man?'

About to say, *no*! Raina hesitated. That would be unfair. Of course he was a good man—she knew he had been good to her. But there was a hardness in him, too, and dangerous depths that she was afraid to try and fathom. 'Logan isn't——' she hesitated. 'Logan isn't husband material,' she said finally.

'Hah!' said Mrs Crimmins sceptically, and Raina laughed.

'Find me another man,' she said lightly, 'and maybe I'll consider it.'

She hardly expected to be taken at her word, but only a few days later, Mrs Crimmins knocked at the door. She was accompanied by a tall, fair man with a pleasant face who turned out to be one of her former foster-children, Robert Linton.

Raina invited them both in, and before they left she had somehow committed herself to having dinner in Hamilton the following Saturday evening with Robert. Mrs Crimmins would look after Danny, she assured them, and gave Raina no chance to change her mind.

Robert was a pleasant escort, friendly and considerate and undemanding. They danced after their dinner, and Raina found herself enjoying it. It seemed a long time since she had been on a dance floor, and Robert was good at it. They didn't stay late, mindful of Mrs Crimmins waiting for them to return, but as the car sped away from the city on the road to Te Ahu, Robert made a sudden exclamation as the vehicle coughed and jerked and finally whined to a halt.

Raina looked at him enquiringly, and he grinned ruefully and said, 'I'm not out of petrol. The tank was filled today.'

She smiled back, not for a moment thinking he had arranged this. The night was too chilly to make cuddling in the car an attractive proposition, anyway, and Robert had more sophistication and maturity than to stage a fake breakdown.

She held the torch for him while he investigated the mysteries of the engine, and obediently turned the key several times while he studied the results under the hood. Another night-time motorist stopped to help, offering a lift if necessary, but he was not going as far as Te Ahu, and although Robert would have asked him to take Raina home, Raina preferred to stay with her escort.

Eventually a petrol blockage was diagnosed, and Robert managed to clear it, but the mishap had kept them for over an hour, so that they were much later arriving home than they had intended.

Robert was apologising for the anti-climactic end to their evening, and Raina laughingly reassured him that she hadn't minded, as they mounted the steps to her front door. She said, 'You'll come in, won't you, have a cup of coffee and see Mrs Crimmins?'

'Thank you. I won't stay long,' he assured her, as she opened the door and stepped inside. 'You've been a honey about all this,' he added, and stooped to drop a light kiss on her lips.

Raina accepted it in the spirit it was meant, a tribute and a thank you. But at that moment the door from the lounge opened, and she gasped with surprise as she saw, not Mrs Crimmins, but Logan standing in the shaft of light from the room behind him.

She started back from Robert's light hold on her shoulder almost guiltily, and was immediately annoyed with herself for having done so. 'What are you doing here?' she demanded crossly, as Robert turned and looked curiously at Logan.

'Waiting for you,' he said curtly. 'Mrs Crimmins expected you back much earlier, didn't she?'

Robert said, 'Yes. We had a breakdown.'

'Oh, yes?' queried Logan, with a fine edge of scepticism in his voice.

Robert looked questioningly at Raina, and she hastily introduced the two men. They didn't shake hands, but nodded to each other, and Logan stepped back into the lounge so that they could follow.

'Where's Mrs Crimmins?' Raina asked Logan.

'I sent her home. I was going to wait for you, anyway, and there was no point in both of us being here.'

'You wanted to see me about something?'

He looked at her and said, 'Obviously. But it can wait—now.'

Until Robert had gone, he meant. She said, 'I was just offering Robert coffee—will you have some?'

'No. I made myself some a little while ago, thanks.'

Robert, looking faintly uncomfortable, said, 'Well, if Mrs Crimmins isn't here, I won't stay for coffee, Raina.' And although she tried to persuade him, knowing he had a long drive back to Hamilton, within five minutes he had driven off, leaving her alone with Logan. She was angry, knowing that Logan had driven him away, and that he had done it deliberately.

She went to the front door with Robert, and after closing it returned to the lounge and said with challenge in her eyes, 'Well?'

Logan was leaning on the mantelpiece over the fire-place where the embers still glowed. He had been ex-amining a bronze model of a tiger moth, turning it in his long fingers. Now he replaced it on the mantel and turned to face her across the room.

'So that's Robert,' he said softly, his tone faintly de-risive.

Raina lifted her eyebrows a little and said, 'Yes. Why do you say it like that?'

'Like what?' he asked, knowing perfectly well.

Raina bit her lip angrily, and he said, 'I've been hear-ing all about him from Mrs Crimmins. He's apparently her blue-eyed boy. Sweet-tempered, biddable and kind to children.'

'They're all good qualities,' she flashed defensively.

'Very. He'd let you walk all over him, and bore you to tears.'

'He's a big boy now,' she reminded him. 'He's hardly likely to let me walk all over him, even if I wanted to.'

'You would. You couldn't help it.'

Stung, she said tightly, 'Thanks! I take it I'm a bossy woman. Did I walk all over Perry, do you think?'

'You loved Perry.'

'Perhaps I could love again,' she said recklessly.

Logan was silent for a long moment, then he said, 'Now there's a thought. Perhaps you could at that. But don't pick on poor Robert.'

'*Poor* Robert? What a charming opinion you have of my character!'

'I have the highest opinion of your character. That's why I can't see you taking Robert seriously.'

Raina was floored by that. It sounded like a back-handed compliment, and she didn't know what she could say. Finally she managed weakly, 'He's very nice.'

'We already agreed on that. Is that what you think you want? A *nice* man?'

He made it sound dull and insipid. She said, 'Perry was a very nice man.'

'Perry was a good deal more than that.'

'Perhaps Robert has hidden depths.'

'You don't want Robert.'

'*I* know what I want!' she said furiously.

Logan had straightened away from the mantelpiece, and was looking at her thoughtfully, hands thrust into his pockets. 'I wonder,' he said. He came towards her, and his hands left his pockets and held her shoulders while he looked down at her.

She tried to move out of his hold, pulling away, but his grasp tightened. 'You let Robert kiss you,' he stated flatly.

'He didn't ask for permission,' she said.

A faint smile touched his mouth. 'Then there's a precedent,' he said, and his mouth came down and claimed her lips under a hard, warm pressure.

She tried to pull away, and his arm curved about her waist, bringing her closer, locking her protesting hands against his chest. One hand encircled her nape, and then began a long, slow, lingering caress of her back, while his mouth continued its determined exploration of hers, finally parting her lips with an insistent demand for surrender.

Her body was curved into his, her head forced back by his kiss. A slow trickle of fire coursed through her, and she suddenly melted into his hard embrace, her mouth eagerly welcoming the erotic greed of his kiss.

But when he moved and pulled her down with him on to the sofa, the dreamlike state into which she had fallen suddenly lifted, and she gasped and struggled out of his arms, standing up with her back to him, because she couldn't bear to look at his face. 'No!' she said, chokingly. 'Go away, Logan!'

He didn't answer, and when she turned reluctantly to face him, he was still on the sofa, sitting across one corner, his arm on the back of it, watching her.

'Come here,' he said softly, and she clenched her teeth and muttered, '*No!* Will you *get out?*'

He stood up then, and she automatically fell back from him. He stayed where he was, standing before the sofa, a faint frown between his brows. 'You're not frightened of me!' he said harshly. 'You're afraid of your own emotions, aren't you? Are you ashamed of responding to me?'

Her face flamed, and she said, 'Will you *please* just go? I've had a long day, and I *want* you *out!*'

'You *want* me, period!' he told her bluntly. 'But you won't admit it. Why——? You can't keep your feelings in cold storage for the rest of your life.'

'What I do with my feelings is my business and no one else's,' she snapped. 'And I don't need your help. I've been offered that kind of—service—before.'

'What? What do you mean?'

'I mean you're not the only man who's made a pass at me, told me I needn't do without sex just because I've lost my husband. I should have known that you weren't any different from the rest, only as Perry's friend, I thought——'

She heard the quick hiss of his breath as he sucked it in, and she plunged on. 'I was wrong, wasn't I? You're no different at all. I'm a widow, and fair game, apparently, for any man. You'd better join the queue, Logan. Not that it will do you any good—I told the rest of them, and I'm telling you, I'm not interested—thanks! Do I make myself clear?'

His eyes were brilliant but hard with anger, and his face looked gaunt.

'You couldn't be clearer,' he said raspingly. 'Get out of my way, Raina—because if I touch you, I'll shake you *senseless*!'

Raina blinked at the violence in his voice, his eyes, and moved aside as he strode past her, wrenched open the front door and slammed it noisily behind him.

CHAPTER THREE

RAINA didn't see Logan after that for more than two weeks. Sometimes she wondered if she had finally driven him away for ever, and was cross with herself because the thought brought a hollow, sickening fear with it. Surely she had not come to rely so much on him? As she was always telling him, she was a grown woman and capable of shouldering her own responsibilities without his help.

But there were times when she found herself standing by the phone, fighting the urge to pick up the receiver and dial the number of Logan's office at the airfield.

In the end, she had to phone him, because Danny's birthday was imminent, and he was insisting that Logan be present at his party. She had arranged for a few of his play-centre friends to join him for a birthday lunch, and hoped that would suffice. But Danny wanted Logan, too. In vain she told him Uncle Logan was busy and might be unable to come. The child was adamant that she at least ask.

When Logan answered her call, she kept her voice cool and brisk, explaining that Danny wanted him at the party, but she would understand and try to reconcile Danny if he couldn't make it.

He said bluntly, 'Is that a polite way of telling me you would prefer me not to come?'

'No!' she answered swiftly.

And before she could add to or qualify that, he said curtly, 'I'll be there. Thanks for the invitation.' And then he hung up.

He was still angry with her, and she was annoyed

that the fact depressed her. She didn't want to care so much for his opinion, for his feelings about her. When he turned up for the party, she was polite and distant, keeping herself too busy to have any conversation with him. He stayed for less than an hour and a half, long enough to satisfy Daniel, and left Raina with a brief word of thanks and a sardonic smile.

She wondered with a sinking heart if he would wait for another invitation before he came again, and told herself grimly that if so, he would wait a very long time. But a few days later he came again, handing her a sheaf of purple and gold irises wrapped in crisp green florist's paper.

She took them and stepped back to let him into the narrow hallway. He had never brought her flowers before, and she must have looked surprised and perhaps a little wary, because he grinned narrowly at her and said, 'A small offering in return for your frequent—if reluctant—hospitality, Raina.'

'Thank you,' she said, stiffly, not bothering to deny the implied accusation. 'You needn't have bothered. We owe you far more than a few meals.'

The grin disappeared, his teeth clamping shut, and she knew she had angered him again. 'You owe me nothing,' he said shortly.

She smiled and shook her head, noting the grim look about her mouth, as she led the way into the lounge where Danny was turning over the pages of a book he had received for his birthday.

As soon as he saw Logan, the boy's face lit up, and he scrambled to his feet, throwing himself at the man in an ecstasy of welcome. 'Uncle Logan! You going to take me in a airplane today?'

'Not today, sport,' Logan answered, going down on his haunches to bring his face level with the child's. 'I have to arrange a suitable day with your mother first.'

'You promised——' Daniel said accusingly.

'Yes, sure. It's all right. I'll take you flying, I just have to explain to Mummy and see what she thinks. But it will be very soon, don't worry.'

Raina had gone suddenly cold, then hot with a furious anger. Before she could stop herself she heard her voice, high and hard, say, 'No, it won't!'

Danny turned an astonished, wide-eyed look on her, and Logan looked up and then slowly straightened, holding her eyes with a narrow, rapier-sharp stare.

She wrenched her own eyes away and said to Danny, 'I'm sorry, darling—you're not old enough yet to go flying with Uncle Logan. Maybe later, when you're bigger——'

'I *am* big!' Danny cried fiercely. 'I *four*! Uncle Logan says I big enough!'

She stooped to put her arms about him. 'Look, darling——'

But he pushed her away, his small fist thudding against her breast and making her wince, then he kicked at her with his foot, his face crimson with rage and his voice piercing as he shouted, 'I *hate* you, Mummy! Uncle Logan *promised*!'

She raised her arm to fend off his flailing hands, and then Logan stepped forward and plucked the boy away, standing him firmly on the carpet in front of him, and holding his shoulders as he said sternly, '*That's enough, now!*'

The temper tantrum subsided abruptly, and Danny looked sullenly at the dark-faced man who held him. Logan had never spoken to him like that before. Tears welled in the child's brown eyes, and Logan said more gently, 'It's all right, son. Maybe it wasn't a good idea to surprise your mother with this. We'll have to give her time to get used to it, okay? And if you want to be treated like a big boy, you have to act like one, you know. Big boys don't hit ladies—no matter what the provocation. Would you like to tell her you're sorry?'

'Not sorry!' Danny muttered, and a slight smile touched the corners of the man's mouth.

'Maybe later, you will be,' he suggested. 'Now why don't you go off to your own room for a while, and let me talk to your mother? Go on, now.'

Danny cast a reproachful, sulky look at Raina, and then moved to obey.

They heard his bedroom door close with a slam as they stood facing each other in the lounge. And then Logan said abruptly, 'What's the problem?'

'You had no right to promise Danny *anything* without asking my permission first!'

'I suppose not,' he said. 'I apologise. But I wanted to give him a birthday treat, and as it wasn't possible to arrange the trip then, I thought I would tell him about it and let him at least have it to look forward to. I would have mentioned it to you, but there didn't seem to be a chance for conversation at his party. And it never crossed my mind that you would have any objection to the idea.'

'Well, I *do*!' she said swiftly.

'Why?' he asked frowningly. 'You don't, surely, think he's too young? At his age, he'll love it!'

'He's *my* son,' she said tightly. 'I don't have to give you reasons.'

Logan made an impatient gesture, and after a moment said, 'You're surely not going to deprive him just because I didn't ask your permission first?'

He was watching her face, and she turned away to avoid his scrutiny, shrugging her shoulders to convey an indifference she didn't feel. 'He can't have everything he wants,' she said.

'Granted. But I don't go back on promises.'

'*I* made no promises,' she said.

'And I didn't have the right,' he conceded wearily. 'We've covered that much. But I don't believe you would make Dan suffer in order to spite *me*—there has to be another reason.'

'My reasons are my own business,' she said in brittle tones.

He ignored that, and she stiffened warily as he said slowly, 'You've never been up, yourself, since Perry died, have you——? Come to think of it, you haven't even come out to the airfield since then.'

She turned to face him, saying quickly, 'That has nothing to do with it.'

'And you turned down a flying job,' he said. 'On the grounds that it's safer behind a desk.'

'Desks don't crash,' she said.

'*I* don't crash, either.'

'That's what Perry used to say.'

There was a short, intense silence. Then Logan said, 'Perry took stupid risks.'

'And you never do?' Raina asked scornfully.

'I've no need to.'

Sensing a criticism of her husband, she lifted her chin and demanded, 'What do you mean by that?'

'Perry was always trying to prove himself,' Logan said. 'You must know that—you lived with him for four years. And you must know as well as I do what drove him into risking his life over and over.'

'*Drove him?*'

He looked back at the shocked challenge in her eyes, and said softly, 'Good God! I don't believe you do.'

'Perry enjoyed taking risks,' she said. 'He seemed to have no sense of fear.'

'Perry laughed in the face of death,' said Logan, 'because he was terrified!'

Raina's eyes blazed disbelief and anger. 'Are you calling Perry a coward? You were his best friend!'

'I'm not calling him a coward—on the contrary, he was incredibly brave—even foolishly so. He wouldn't let his fears beat him, and he always had more guts than sense, even as a child. The first time I remember seeing him, he was trying to fight off two boys bigger than himself—ineffectually, but with determination. He knew he was going to be beaten, but he would go down fighting.'

'But you came to the rescue,' she said. 'He told me about it.'

'Did he? Is that how he put it?'

'More or less. You were his hero, weren't you? You must have enjoyed that.'

'I was his friend. Perry always needed someone strong behind him. That's why he married you.'

'*What?*' Raina found she was trembling, and clenched her hands at her sides. 'He wasn't a weakling!'

'I don't mean that he was!'

'I think you *do* mean that! How can you—you're despicable! He would never have said a word against *you*!'

'Being his friend doesn't mean I have to see him through rose-coloured spectacles. I loved him as he was.'

'I'll bet!' she said sarcastically. 'Did his admiration for you reinforce your sense of superiority? Did you enjoy despising him?'

Almost violently, Logan insisted, 'I *didn't* despise him! I admired his courage, and his gaiety, I enjoyed his humour and had a great respect for his talents. I was grateful for his friendship. As a child, I was a loner, a big kid who was expected to live up to his size, rather than his age, and resented it. I took life too seriously and had a chip on my shoulder. Perry helped to humanise me.'

Raina couldn't resist a sceptical raising of her eyebrows, and Logan stopped speaking, and laughed.

The laughter eased the angry tension between them, and when he spoke again his voice had softened. 'Believe me,' he said, 'I'm not trying to put Perry down. He meant a great deal to me.'

'I know.'

'And so does his son,' Logan added quietly.

Raina tensed.

Logan went on deliberately, 'Perry loved flying, Raina. It scared him, but he loved it. He would have taken Dan up before now, *wouldn't he?*'

'You don't know that.'

'Yes, I do. And so do you. Don't impose your own fears on Daniel.'

'Fears?' she repeated, her voice sharp.

'That's why you don't want him to go with me, isn't it? You can't forget how his father died.'

'That has——'

'Everything to do with it, I think!' he said confidently. 'But you won't admit it to me. Never mind—but let me take Dan up—for Perry's sake.'

Raina fought a short, bitter battle with herself, and finally said reluctantly, 'All right, Logan. For Perry's sake.'

'It will only be a short flight,' he said. 'I'll be very careful.'

Raina nodded, her mouth tight.

'I can make it tomorrow,' he said. 'If you could bring him out to the airfield—after lunch?'

She had thought he would pick Danny up himself. For a moment she wanted to protest, make some excuse not to be there. Then she saw the watchful look in his eyes, and lifted her chin as she said steadily, 'Okay. Fine.'

Logan murmured something that sounded like, 'Good girl,' but she didn't ask him to repeat it.

Danny received the news ecstatically, of course, and showed a touching remorse for his earlier violence. Raina suppressed a forlorn hope that the next day would prove unsuitable for flying, and made a creditable attempt to join in Danny's rapturous greeting of the warm spring day.

She drove to the airfield making a conscious effort not to remember all the other times she had driven the same route, alongside Perry or on her way to meet him. The rolling hills were brilliantly emerald in the sun, with the lush growth of spring grass on them, and the blossoms were already giving way to new leaves on some of the fruit trees in farm orchards along the way. White manuka blossom dusted some of the uncultivated slopes like a light fall of snow, and the calves and lambs in the neatly fenced paddocks at the roadside switched their tails and danced away on sturdy legs as the car passed.

They descended on to flat land formed by an ancient, long-dried river bed and its adjacent swamps that had been drained and turned into rich farm land, and then Danny called excitedly that he could see the airplanes.

There were three of them parked near the big hangars, and a helicopter sat like a huge squat dragonfly a little apart from the others. The single-wing planes were not big, but small craft with two seats, designed for top-dressing on the hilly farmlands of New Zealand. The specially built aircraft, with their large tanks in the fuselage for fertiliser, crop sprays or weedkiller, and their easy loading and discharging features, were a far cry from the early Tiger Moths left over from wartime which the first 'supermen' had used to spread superphosphate from the air on infertile land, bringing, eventually, millions of barren acres into production. These were handy, strong, easily manoeuvred machines, made for safe take-off and landing on short, sometimes rough and often sloping runways devised by farmers who might not have much flat, smooth land. When the planes were not working, the runway would be grazed by stock, and from Perry and Logan, Raina had heard hair-raising stories of their own topdressing days, when sheep might have to be cleared from the runway before each take-off, and had been known to stray back on again when the plane was about to land on its homeward run.

Sheep were not the only hazard for the pilots in the business of agricultural flying. Perry had always maintained that his ability to fly a plane under high-tension power wires was a necessary skill. In the back country a pilot sometimes found wires which he had not known about, and had to take quick evasive action to save himself and his plane. Wires were not easily seen against the ground, and the agricultural pilots normally flew low over the land to drop their loads in the right places. A passenger was sometimes carried especially to watch out for wires which might entangle an aircraft. Then there were the inherent dangers of the countryside itself, and the low angle of the flight paths. For a pilot following the contour of a hillside in order to spread his load efficiently, a momentary distraction could be enough to bring his aircraft to a lethal angle in relation to the steep terrain.

And there were all the things that might go wrong during take-off and landing procedures, acknowledged as the most hazardous stages of any flight. Since agricultural flights averaged twelve to fifteen of these every hour, the accident rate tended to look very high, although Perry had said that New Zealand's record was good compared with the rest of the world.

The sight of the planes on the ground, the silver corrugated iron hangars, the long, low modern office building, brought Perry's memory vividly back, and for a few minutes Raina found herself racked by a pain as acute as in the first weeks after his death.

But Danny was excitedly pulling at her arm as soon as she parked the car at the rear of the building, and she blinked away stinging tears to smile at him, thrusting the memories back to concentrate on his happy chatter.

Inside there was a new girl on the reception desk, a pretty, composed blonde who glanced at them with impersonal enquiry, and gave a cool professional smile when Raina explained who she was and that Logan was expecting them.

'I'll tell him you're here, Mrs Kimball,' she said, and disappeared into the inner office. Logan and Perry had used to share it, and Raina would have breezed past the friendly middle-aged receptionist, merely enquiring if anyone was with one of the partners, before going in.

When the blonde girl returned and ushered them in, Raina glanced around with surprise. The two wooden tables which had served as desks in Perry's time had been removed, and instead a large shiny laminated desk occupied much of the floor space. New filing cabinets were topped by healthy-looking green plants, and the shabby carpet square had been replaced by a deep-pile wall-to-wall floor covering. Logan rose from a large dark leather swivel chair behind the vast desk, and came round to welcome them, pulling forward an armchair in matching leather for Raina.

He didn't go back to his own seat, but leaned on the edge of the desk with his arms folded, watching her.

'You don't approve?' he asked, looking round at the changed appearance of the room.

'It's—very nice.'

Logan grimaced. 'Damned with faint praise,' he said mockingly. Then, his gaze sharpening, he said, 'Does it—bother you?'

It did, terribly. Raina was conscious of an illogical feeling of outrage. Nothing of Perry remained in this room, nothing of the casual, welcoming atmosphere of a small firm and a friendly partnership which had pervaded the place before. She looked at the expensive textured covering on the walls that she recalled used to be covered with charts, plans, the odd calendar, and cryptic notes on designs, orders and problems to be overcome. Now there was one chart pulled down from a neat pelmet on the wall that housed several more rolled up like blinds. Very efficient, no doubt. And beside it—she stared and then leaned forward as she saw the photograph. It was the only thing left that had been part of the clutter in the old office, when it had been fixed to the wall by four rusting drawing pins, and sometimes half hidden by the other bits of paper surrounding it. Now it was framed to match the pelmet—a photograph of Perry and Logan standing outside the huge, shabby old shed in which they had first started their business, with their first and then only plane parked outside.

She got up and went over to look at it, and after a moment she felt Logan put his hands on her shoulders, standing behind her. Daniel, moved by curiosity, followed them, and as Raina put her own hand on his childish shoulder, he said, 'That's you, Uncle Logan—and my daddy.'

'That's right,' Logan said quietly. 'I insisted that it had to stay, fancy frame or no. I wouldn't part with it.'

He was talking to her, Raina knew, not to Danny.

She moved slightly, and his hands dropped. 'I expect the office was overdue for redecoration,' she said lightly, returning to her seat, where Danny leaned against her knees, playing with the folds of her skirt.

'Angela thought so,' said Logan.

'Angela?'

'My new secretary,' he explained, with a movement of his head towards the outer office. 'She was horrified at the squalor I worked in—said it was bad for the image.'

'I thought the office in Hamilton was the one where your public relations came into play,' she said. There was a small sales office there, complete with carpet and pot plants, but this one had always been the working centre of the business, the place where the decisions were made and put into practice. She had never thought of it as 'squalid' but as homely and comfortable, and work-manlike.

'We have more and more clients coming out here to inspect the new machines and try them,' Logan explained. 'We got an order from Thailand that I told you about—had to entertain a high-ranking Thai official and take him up for a trial flight. I must admit that this——' he waved a hand at their surroundings '——must have created a better impression than the old version would have.'

'I suppose so.' Raina sounded slightly dry. 'Did Angela choose the décor?'

His glance might have held a trace of amusement. 'Yes,' he said.

'She must be a gem. Secretary and interior decorator. What else does she do?'

She spoke lightly, but there was a brief, telling silence, and Logan's eyes flashed a warning signal before he said, equally lightly, 'A lot. Secretaries like her are hard to find.'

'I'm sure,' Raina murmured, her smile sweetly understanding.

Softly, he said, 'You're barking up the wrong tree, Raina.'

She flushed slightly, but Danny created a diversion, having tired of waiting for the grown-ups to complete their incomprehensible conversation. 'I want to go plane now!' he announced, and Logan grinned and said, 'Okay, Dan. Come ,outside and I'll find a plane for us.'

The single-engine two-seater looked terribly small and fragile, but Danny went aboard without a qualm, and trustingly waited for 'Uncle Logan' to join him. Raina fixed a frozen smile to her face and waved as the aircraft taxied to the runway, and kept waving as it gathered speed and took off, because she knew Danny would be watching for her, eager for her to see him on his great adventure.

But as the plane gained height and banked into a turn at the end of the runway, she lowered her hand, and sank down on a nearby crate, wiping sweat from her palms on her skirt, fighting down a wave of nausea induced by terror.

The plane flew out of sight, and it seemed an eternity before it returned. She watched with aching eyes as it swept low over the airfield, then turned on to finals for landing. She was watching so intently that she didn't notice when the girl Angela came out of the office and walked over to stand nearby.

The small plane touched down beautifully, a sleek, perfectly smooth landing, and Raina let her taut body sag a little with relief.

'Are you all right, Mrs Kimball?' a cool feminine voice enquired, and she straightened and turned to meet a pair of curious blue eyes.

'Quite all right, thank you,' she returned, equally coolly. 'It's just a bit boring, waiting for them, that's all.'

She watched the plane taxi to a standstill, and then Logan's tall figure jumped out, and turned to lift out Danny's small one.

Danny ran ahead to his mother, words tumbling over each other in his excited anxiety to describe every moment of the flight, and the three adults listened for some minutes, Logan and his secretary standing side by side, and Raina, still seated on the crate, with her arm about her son and her eyes fixed with loving attention on his animated little face.

When he finally ran out of description, Logan said, 'Well, sport, we've another little surprise for you. I've been keeping a chocolate icecream sundae in the fridge, just for you. Sounds good?'

'*Yeah!*'

'Good. Well, Angela will take you inside and find it for you—and it's your mother's turn to go for a ride in an airplane.'

Raina felt momentarily winded. She raised startled eyes to his and protested, 'No! I don't want——'

But his hand was on her arm, firm and insistent. And Danny was saying, 'I'll wave to you, Mummy. I saw you waving at *me*.'

'I don't think——' Raina stammered, hating Logan and panicking at the thought of climbing into the tiny cockpit and flying for the first time since the terrible day of Perry's accident.

'Come on,' he said implacably. And then, very softly, 'Don't let Dan down, Raina.'

He knew—he *knew*! And he had planned this deliberately, to force her in front of Danny so that she couldn't back out. This was why he had asked her to bring Danny herself.

'I'll look after Dan, Mrs Kimball,' said Angela in her polite, composed voice, and suddenly that was part of it too, the fact that this girl was watching her with curiosity in her eyes and a faint smile on her carefully reddened mouth, while her hand held Danny's small one, and she called him Dan. As Logan did.

Raina took a deep, quick breath and began to walk beside Logan, her eyes glassy with the effort not to scream and run, her legs working stiffly as she neared the silver-bodied plane and pictures danced before her eyes of the other one, so like this, broken and twisted and torn, and with the broken, torn body of her husband fatally trapped inside it.

Logan helped her into the cockpit, murmuring something she was too disturbed to hear. Automatically she fumbled for her seat belt, and then he was climbing in beside her, checking his instruments, closing the cockpit, locking the two of them into the tiny space.

She heard him say clearly, 'Relax, Raina. Trust me.'

She didn't look at him, or answer. And after a minute or two the engine rumbled as he opened the throttle, and her nerves tightened still further as she felt the vibration in the cockpit.

Her teeth bit into her lower lip as the plane trundled to the runway, and when Logan said quietly, 'Wave to Dan—he's watching you,' she turned her head stiffly to focus rather desperately on the small figure in the distance, her hand moving jerkily in reply to the little boy's enthusiastic gesture.

She closed her eyes as the aircraft gained momentum and her heart turned over as the familiar drag and lift came when they left the ground. When she opened her eyes they were cruising steadily, the land below them a tapestry of green intersected by darker greens, a ribbon of grey road winding over the hills, and the roofs of oddly squat-looking farmhouses lending accents of brighter colours in red or orange, or blending into the landscape in brown or green.

From the air, the horizon had expanded, and gradually she relaxed as remembered sensations of strangely mingled peace and exhilaration replaced her fear and panic.

Logan flew on in silence, apparently ignoring her, but he must have sensed what was happening. He banked the plane at last into a turn back towards the airfield, then said, 'Take the controls, Raina.'

For a moment she sat frozen, all her fear returning in a cold, sickening wave of terror. Then his voice said again, steady and hard, 'Take the controls.'

She steadied herself, and took over from him, her eyes automatically flicking over the instrument panel, checking their height and airspeed, and her hand reaching for the dual control column in front of her.

The airfield came into view, and she glanced enquiringly at Logan, who nodded decisively, his face expressionless but his cool blue eyes watchful, and Raina began to ease the machine into a downward leg, heading for the runway.

The landing was not quite what it should have been, because just at touchdown she had a momentary picture of Perry's plane as it hit the ground and disintegrated, and her hand jerked on the control, making the plane bounce. Biting her lip, she eased back on the control column and closed the throttle until the wheels finally touched down, then carefully applied the brakes, bringing them eventually to a gentle halt.

When Logan helped her down out of the cockpit, his face was still expressionless, but he kept his hands on her waist for a moment, and said quietly, 'All right?'

'Yes,' she said. And then, because she owed it to him, she added with an effort, 'Thank you, Logan.'

He didn't reply to that, but a faint hint of a smile touched his mouth as he released her. Her legs felt a bit wobbly with reaction as they walked together back to the buildings, and she wondered if she was a little pale—she felt it—but she walked steadily enough, and she wasn't faint.

Daniel was sitting in a chair in the outer office, a paper napkin tucked about his neck, and his face smeared with the chocolate icecream he was enjoying, scooping out the contents of an enormous paper tub with a blue plastic spoon.

Angela was seated at the typewriter, and she looked up and smiled with more warmth than Raina had seen yet. She wondered if the warmth was directed at Logan.

'All over?' she asked, with one of those curious blue glances of hers at Raina, who deduced that Logan had confided his plan to the girl, and found the thought distinctly unwelcome. She didn't want to be an object of curiosity or pity to Logan's—secretary.

'All over,' said Logan. 'How about a cup of tea, Angel?'

Angel? Raina cast a deliberately sardonic look at Logan as he took her arm to guide her into his own office, and he returned it with an amused raising of his eyebrows, and a slight grin.

She resisted the pressure on her arm, looking at Danny, but Logan said, 'He's hardly noticed that we're back. We won't disturb him.'

It was true, Danny had scarcely glanced up when they entered, intent on making the most of his treat. Raina smiled resignedly and allowed Logan to steer her to the chair she had occupied before.

This time, however, Logan remained standing, and

when she looked up at him with enquiry, he moved abruptly away from her to stand at the window behind the desk, turning his rather harsh profile to her as he looked out across the airfield. He asked, without looking at her, 'Does it hurt, coming here?'

'Yes,' she said.

'You did ask me for a job.'

'I know. I could have worked in the Hamilton office.'

'Is that what you thought? You would have had to come here, some time.'

'Yes. I thought I'd cross that bridge when I came to it.'

'Well, now you have. Are you sorry?'

'No.'

He turned then to give her a penetrating look. 'The first few weeks,' he told her, 'it hurt like hell every time I walked in here. I think that's why——' he hesitated, glancing around the room, and she realised what he meant. The redecorating had erased some of the reminders. A little of her own hurt eased then, even as he said, 'The pain doesn't last for ever. Not with the same—intensity.'

Raina thought of the way she had felt when she arrived here this afternoon, and perhaps the shadow of it showed in her face. Logan moved away suddenly from the window, his hand gripping the back of the chair that stood behind the desk. 'That *must* be true for you, too,' he said. 'Life——'

'Goes on?' she said ironically, completing the cliché. 'Oh, yes—after a fashion.'

'Don't talk like that!' he said forcefully, and then his eyes moved past her, and the harshness in his face relaxed as he said, 'Hi, Dan. Finished your sundae?'

The little boy came into the room, and Raina turned to hold out her hand, take the napkin from his neck and wipe his face and hands with it. He still clutched the empty tub, and Logan reached over and took it from him to drop it into a wastebasket standing beside the desk. 'I think you need a wash, sport,' he said. 'Come with me.'

Raina sat back in the chair as they went out, the man's hand resting lightly on the boy's head. She had the odd conviction that Logan had seized on the excuse to leave her for a few minutes, that he somehow felt a need to get away.

Angela brought a tray in and placed it on the desk. Tea and biscuits, the teacups flowered and dainty and unchipped, with a matching jug and sugar basin. Raina remembered tea-stained pottery mugs and the sugar presented in a cup that had lost its handle. 'That looks very nice,' she said, with hollow sincerity. 'Thank you.'

The girl smiled and went out again, and Raina heard the electric typewriter in the outer office begin its staccato tattoo.

She was pouring the tea when Logan and Danny came back. Logan lifted up the boy to sit on the desk top, and took the cup she handed him. She flicked a glance at his face and found no sign of any discomposure. He sat in his chair and leaned back in relaxed fashion as he sipped the hot liquid, his eyes on the boy, who had picked up a glass paperweight with a downy thistle head miraculously trapped inside, and was examining it with absorption.

'How is it done?' Raina asked.

Logan said, 'I've no idea. I guess it's a trade secret.'

'Did you buy it overseas?'

'No, I believe they're made locally. It was given to me.'

He didn't say who had given it, and she didn't ask.

She finished her tea, rescued the glass bauble as it

slipped in her son's hands, and carefully replaced it on the desk as she said, 'Well, thank you for everything, Logan. We must be going.'

She lifted Daniel down as Logan rose to his feet, his 'Don't mention it,' holding a hint of mockery. She looked away from him, admonishing Danny to add his own thanks to hers. He did so readily enough, and then Logan went out with them to the car.

He closed the door on them, then put a hand on the frame of the open window and leaned down to say, 'How about a trip to the beach next Sunday, you two? The weather is looking up lately.'

Danny wriggled with anticipatory joy as he endorsed the suggestion, and Raina shot a look of exasperated anger at Logan. 'I'll think about it,' she said.

His voice low, Logan said, 'For Dan's sake, Raina.'

'Don't *push* me, Logan,' she whispered fiercely. 'I won't submit to blackmail.'

'It isn't blackmail, it's an invitation.'

'You know what I mean.'

'Don't cut off Danny's nose to spite your face.'

She took a quick, angry breath. 'Danny can go if he likes.'

'The invitation was for two of you.'

Sensing a disagreement, Danny began to whine, tugging at her arm. Resolutely, Raina ignored him, her eyes clashing with Logan's. 'You mean you won't take him if I don't come, too?'

Logan shrugged. 'If you like.'

'*Is* that what you meant?' she demanded, over Danny's increasing importunities.

Logan looked past her at the child and said, 'Stop it, Dan! Be quiet, or I won't take you anywhere!'

The whining abruptly ceased, and Raina experienced a not unfamiliar sense of irritation, because Danny always took notice of Logan, where such an admonition from her would have had little effect.

'Well?' Logan demanded. 'Is it yes or no?'

She glanced down at Danny and saw his eyes enormous and hopeful, and his cheeks red with the effort of holding back his entreaties. He looked at her, and his mouth trembled a little. Defeated, she turned to Logan and said, 'Yes.'

'I'll pick you up at eight-thirty,' he said. 'Don't worry about food, I'll bring something.'

He stepped back, and she didn't look at him again as she started the car and drove off. But the relieved smile on Danny's face almost made the capitulation worthwhile.

CHAPTER FOUR

TE AHU was inland, and to reach the sea they had to drive over the Kaimai range of mountains, climbing away from the plains and foothills up into the wilder reaches of slopes where dark bush plants clung together, fighting one another for sunlight and a foothold, on nearly sheer drops to narrow valleys far below where rivers rilled over smooth-worn grey stones. Sometimes the bush gave way to plantations of tall, dark-needled exotic pines marching away up the hillsides in orderly rows, or to tough grasses grazing sheep on land reclaimed from the bush and from the shrubby manuka.

On the summit the remnants of a morning mist remained, dewing the windscreen and giving the landscape an almost eerie quality of stillness. It lifted as they began the descent, and revealed a vista of distant green under a blue, clear morning sky, with clouds sheeting some of the valleys in soft dense white, so that they seemed to be travelling in a kind of suspension between heaven and earth.

The Bay of Plenty abounded in beautiful beaches, from the pounding surf of Waihi in its northern reaches to the soothing calm of sheltered inlets along the coast where rivers joined the sea, and the long sweep of white, tide-washed sand at Ohope near Whakatane.

At Tauranga the harbour was enclosed by a long flat peninsula ending in 'The Mount'—properly called Maunganui, a graceful hill that presided over one of the most popular beach resorts in the country.

Raina was glad that Logan had chosen to take them here, to Ocean Beach, where even this early in the season the warm day had brought out a fair crowd of people to enjoy the sand and the gentle surf. It was a little cool for swimming in the sea, but the heated saltwater pools at the foot of The Mount were ideal for a dip after a session at the marineland. Danny had watched with fascinated glee the performance of seals, sea-lions and penguins as their keepers put them through a variety of acts.

After their swim they had a late lunch at a picnic spot overlooking the harbour, where pleasure boats danced about, dwarfed by the giant container ships which kept the port busy; and the city of Tauranga on the farther shore sprawled up into the hills and down to the sea's edge.

Logan had brought a whole cold roasted chicken, slices of ham, buttered bread rolls and salads in plastic containers. There was also fizzy lemonade for Danny and a bottle of white wine in a special cooler for the two adults.

Raina raised her brows at the wine, and said dryly, 'Heavens! Wine for a picnic?'

Logan grinned down at her as he deftly removed the cork, and asked, 'Would you prefer the traditional black tea from a billy?'

'I don't think anyone boils up a billy these days, do they?' she said lightly. 'I think most people use thermos flasks.'

'You have to admit this has more class than a thermos.' He had produced two stemmed glasses and was carefully filling them and then handing one to her.

'I never suspected you of having class, Logan.'

He put down the tall green glass bottle and lifted his glass to hers, his eyes laughing at her. 'I try,' he said gravely, with completely false humility, and Raina bit her lip to stop laughter from escaping.

Sipping his wine, he looked at her curiously over the rim of the glass. As he lowered it, she looked away and tasted her own drink. It was cool and sharp, immediately recognisable as a superior wine. It didn't surprise her—Logan didn't deal in inferior products, he would insist on the best. He had class, all right.

'Why don't you let it out?' he said softly, leaning closer to her, turning his shoulder a little to Danny so that she could see only himself. 'Are you frightened even to *laugh* with me?'

She looked down at her glass, and murmured, 'I don't know what you're talking about.'

'You do,' he argued, keeping his voice low, but it vibrated with some tightly controlled emotion—anger or irritation. Then, almost savagely, he said, his lips barely moving, 'One day I'll get past those barriers of yours, if I have to beat them down!'

Her eyes rose to his in surprise and sudden fear, and he added in a fierce whisper, 'Don't look like that!'

For a moment their eyes locked, and Raina saw a strange expression in his which she was unable to inter-'
pret. Then abruptly he turned away to say something to Danny in quite a different tone.

After they had packed up the picnic he drove the car down to the beach, and they sat for a while parked facing the rolling ocean, the spray spuming off the hurled waves as a few surf-riders rode the crests, and some hardy swimmers dived into the curves racing towards the sand. A family party was chasing a ball and a few couples strolled along the water's edge.

They sat in silence, watching, and Raina found the soothing effect of the ocean almost hypnotic.

- At the same time, she was conscious of the man beside her, his eyes also on the sea, his strong hand resting idly on the curve of the steering wheel, and muscular thighs in casual jeans almost touching hers. In the back seat, Danny was strangely quiet, and when she turned to look at him, the reason was apparent. He had curled up in a corner of the comfortable seat, and dozed off.

Logan looked, too, half turning, with his hand on the back of his own seat, and when he looked back again at Raina his fingers slid forward, until they almost touched her cheek. She moved slightly away from him, and saw the almost familiar anger light the ice blue of his eyes.

'Shall we go for a walk on the beach?' he murmured. Raina glanced at Danny, and Logan said, 'We'll keep the car in sight.'

Danny wouldn't be likely to wake, she knew. And even if he did, he wouldn't be worried. He was familiar with Logan's car, had been on several outings with him, alone. And she didn't want to be confined here with Logan any longer. He was too close, too big, too—*aware.*

'Yes,' she said, and before she could find the handle of the door he had leaned over, his shoulder pressing on hers as he opened the catch for her.

Raina scrambled out, and he closed the door behind her. She watched Danny's sleeping face as Logan got out and closed his own door. The child didn't stir. Logan bent to glance at him, too, and then came round to her side and put a hand on her arm.

The sand was warmed by the sun, and soft underfoot. Raina pulled her arm from Logan's light grip, and stooped to remove her sandals, liking to walk barefoot on the beach, and rolled up the legs of her jeans to mid-calf.

He put out his hand for the shoes, but she shook her head, carrying them herself. Logan looked faintly sardonic, his firm mouth turning down slightly at one corner, but he said nothing.

They walked in silence, strolling along the firm dark strip just above the wavelets that smoothed glassily up the beach, foaming at the edges. Scattered shells were embedded in the sand, and Raina stooped to pick up a speckled trumpet-shaped one, which had survived its journey to shore undamaged.

'Give it to me,' said Logan. 'I'll put it in my pocket.'

'I have a pocket,' she returned coolly, and stowed it away herself.

'You surprise me,' he said. 'Those things fit you so well, I didn't think you could get anything into the pockets.'

Her jeans were snug and neatly fitted, but not tight. Raina flushed faintly and he gave a soft laugh. 'No comeback?' he jeered gently.

'Was that a criticism?' she asked. 'You think my clothes are too tight?'

'No. It was not a criticism, and I like your clothes the way they are. Do you want to know why?'

'No!' Raina answered hastily, and Logan laughed aloud this time. 'Coward!' he taunted. 'Why not?'

'Maybe I know already.'

'Maybe you do,' he drawled. 'And what are you going to do about it—keep on ignoring it?'

'It's too nice a day to get—intense—about things,' she said. 'We should be turning back. Danny might wake up.'

He made an exasperated sound under his breath, but when she turned he followed her, his hands in his pockets, and between his brows a faint frown.

Danny wasn't awake, but he stirred when he heard them return, and was soon sitting up, flushed with sleep, and demanding to be allowed to build a sandcastle.

Logan took a brand new bucket and spade from the trunk of the car, and Danny was soon happily engaged

in excavating an enormous amount of sand, having rejected grown-up help. Raina sat nearby on a towel
Logan had spread for her, and, nodding towards the
shiny spade and bright plastic bucket, she said, 'Thank
you, Logan. You think of everything, don't you?'

He didn't answer, but looked slightly impatient. 'I
think I'll have a swim,' he said, and went off to change.

Raina tried to keep her attention concentrated on
Danny, but when Logan entered the water, she found
her eyes drawn to the tall, tanned figure plunging into
the surf with strong, powerful strokes of his arms, and
watching for the dark head as he dived under a breaker
and reappeared moments later.

When he came out, she knew that he was striding
towards her, picking up his towel and rubbing at his
face, arms and hair as he walked.

She kept her eyes on her son, who now had a broad,
sloping castle built and was busily making tunnels at its
base. Logan flung his towel down beside her and then
followed it, stretching out at full length, so that she had
to look across him to see Danny. His chest was brown
and smooth, his hips lean in brief swimming gear, and
his long legs were straight and muscular, though not
excessively so. He wasn't a hairy man, but the body hair
he had was dark like that on his head, and showed wetly
against his damp skin. Fleetingly, Raina recalled seeing
Perry lie beside her like this after a swim, and how the
hair on his legs and arms, and the faint down on his
chest, had glinted in the sunlight.

She moved restlessly, and Logan glanced at her and
said, 'Something wrong?'

Raina shook her head, but got up and strolled over
to Danny, stooping to inspect the tunnel he had dug
into the castle's base, and asking him what he was
planning to do next.

'A bridge,' he announced firmly, and she looked about for a piece of flat driftwood and presented it to him, saying, 'Will this do?'

He nodded, and proceeded to dig a moat about the castle, using a black mussel shell, instead of his spade. 'Why don't you use the spade?' she asked, and he gave her a scornful, pitying look and said, 'It too big!'

'Oh, yes,' she acknowledged ruefully. Evidently his sense of proportion was strong. She wondered if it meant he was particularly intelligent, then smiled to herself at her own maternal pride.

An elderly couple making their way up from the beach stopped and admired the castle, and the woman pulled a toothpick with a triangle of paper on it from her bag and offered it to Danny for a flag.

It had 'Cheese and Onion' written on it, but Danny didn't mind, and thanked her with a beaming smile, after Raina gently reminded him of his manners.

'I picked it up at lunch, to give to one of my grandchildren,' the woman said to Raina. 'But it would be perfect for a sandcastle. What a lovely little boy! He takes after his mother, doesn't he? Not your husband——!' Her eyes went past Raina to where Logan was lounging now on one elbow, watching them. Raina automatically followed her glance, catching a devilish amusement in Logan's blue eyes as they met hers. He had obviously heard.

There was no point in embarking on a totally unnecessary explanation and embarrassing a perfect stranger, so she bit her tongue and listened glassy-eyed as the woman went on to describe her own grandchildren's various family likenesses, until her husband became impatient and urged her away.

The castle was ready to be decorated with shells, and Danny graciously invited the two adults to help, now that the major part of the construction was done. Logan joined in with lazy tolerance, and Raina avoided his eyes as she collected shells and helped Danny to make patterns with them until he was satisfied, and ready to crown the edifice with the flag the 'nice lady' had given him.

They took another walk along the beach, this time with Danny between them, at first, holding their hands, then darting up and down the beach and happily handing shells and seaweed and driftwood to Logan to 'keep for me'. Logan obliged without protest, pushing the bits and pieces into his pockets, but he drew the line at half a dead crab, and persuaded the child to leave the smelly fragment where it was.

Later they found a rock pool, and Danny watched absorbed as a hermit crab half emerged from its shell and made its way across the bottom of the pool, and tiny fish darted about from one waving seaweed frond to another, disappearing into the background as soon as they stopped moving.

'All gone!' exclaimed Danny with astonishment, and Logan grinned and explained the principles of camouflage. 'Here,' he said. 'See this little flower, Dan?'

He pointed to a sea anemone with its 'petals' gently moving in the clear water of the pool.

'Yes.'

'Well, it isn't a flower at all. Actually, it's an animal pretending to be a flower. That's so that it can catch fish—like this, see?' Logan touched the 'petals' with his little finger, and Danny gave a squeal and then laughed aloud as the anemone closed itself.

Logan pulled his hand away, and Danny demanded, 'Does it hurt, Uncle Logan?'

'No. Do you want to try?'

They found some more anemones, and Danny giggled

as he touched them and felt them tickling his finger as they closed. Then he lifted a hermit crab and laughed as the animal retracted itself into the shell.

'Crabs are funny!' he declared.

Logan said, 'Not only crabs, sport. Sometimes people grow a protective shell, too, and they can be even harder to winkle out of them than crabs.'

'*People* don't have shells!' Danny chortled, evidently convinced that Logan was making a hilarious mistake.

But Logan's eyes were on Raina, and she didn't think he was joking. 'Some do,' he said quietly.

As they walked back to the car, Danny looked at Maunganui, its rounded cone rising from the end of the broad sandspit, and said, 'Mount must be lonely.'

Raina smiled, and Logan said, 'Funny you should say that. Do you want to hear a story about the mountain?'

'Silly question,' Raina murmured dryly. Danny never turned down a story.

Danny listened solemnly as Logan told the ancient Maori legend of a mountain that had once resided at the foot of the mighty Kaimai range, as a young and vigorous hillock which fell in love with a comely nearby female mountain. Spurned by his love, he decided to walk to the sea and drown himself.

'Mountains can't walk!' Danny objected sternly.

'They could, then,' Logan asserted. 'According to the story,' he added, as Raina shot an amused glance at him. 'But only at night. Once the morning came, they had to stay put. Well, this mountain travelled all night, and arrived at the sea's edge with the dawn. And as he hesitated there at the end of the sandspit, the sun rose, so there he had to stay.'

'Is that the end?' Danny demanded.

'Yes. There he stands to this day.' Logan pointed to Maunganui before them.

Danny looked thoughtfully at the mountain, then scampered over the sand and across the grass above the beach to the car.

Logan looked quizzically at Raina and said, 'Didn't he think much of the story?'

'I don't know,' she answered truthfully. 'Maybe he finds it a little difficult to comprehend—a moving mountain.'

'It happens all the time,' Logan assured her. 'There was this guy called Mahomet——'

Raina laughed. She saw him smiling back at her, and caught something in his eyes that flared, making her breath stick in her throat. Then they reached the car, and she devoted her attention to getting some of the sand off her son before he climbed into the back seat again.

'Another story, Uncle Logan!' he demanded, bouncing a little on the leather upholstery.

Raina said automatically, 'Please, Uncle Logan!'

Logan grinned at her and said, 'You, too?' under Danny's obedient echo of the phrase.

She smiled faintly and shook her head. Logan half turned in the seat, to look back at Danny. 'Let's see——' he said thoughtfully. 'Would you like a true story?'

'Yes! Please,' Danny said hastily.

'Okay—your mother will appreciate this one. There was a beautiful young princess who lived around here, about a hundred and fifty years ago, when the Maori tribes were at war with each other. Her name was Te Aho-o-te-Rangi. Her tribe, the Ngai-te-Rangi, lived on the Tauranga side of the harbour—over there——' he pointed, and Danny's eyes followed his pointing finger with interest.

'One night the *pa* was attacked by a great army from another tribe, and after a pretty fierce battle, the attackers set the place on fire. Te Aho, the princess, had a baby son, and to save him she tied him on to her back and began to swim with him all the way to the other side of the harbour—over here. She was seen, and one of the enemy warriors shot her and wounded her, but she managed to swim all the way, and eventually reached her friends on the farther shore, who pulled her from the water and looked after her son, who grew to be a big strong fellow.'

'Did he kill the bad man that shot his mummy?' Danny asked interestedly.

'I expect he had a jolly good try, anyway,' Logan grinned. 'That's how they worked it in those days.'

'Good!' Danny said with satisfaction, and Raina laughed protestingly and said, 'Maybe he forgave the man, and made friends with him. A lot of Maoris became Christians in those days, and learned to forgive their enemies instead of looking for revenge.'

Logan started the engine and said, 'Yes. A pity some of the *pakeha* didn't take more notice of their own white missionaries.'

Under cover of the engine's noise, Raina asked, 'What happened to Te Aho?'

'She died of her wounds, once her son was safe.' He gave her an odd glance and said with some deliberation, 'She gave her life for her child.'

Raina would have done the same, of course, and he knew it. That was why he had said she would appreciate it.

'Don't you approve?' she asked, mindful of that strange note of deliberation in his voice.

'In her case, she had little choice—her son would have been killed or enslaved,' he said. 'I don't go along with unnecessary sacrifices.'

Rather sharply, she said, 'And *you* are the judge of what's necessary?'

His sideways smile was rueful. '*You* won't allow that, will you?' He was turning the car, driving to the main road, his eyes fixed ahead.

'Not if you're applying your judgment to me,' she said steadily.

'Don't you think that sometimes an outsider can see more clearly——?'

'But you're not an outsider,' she said. 'You're——'

'What?' he prompted her. 'An interested party? Okay, maybe I'm biased. Mrs Crimmins isn't.'

Raina's look was startled, then wary. He and Mrs Crimmins must have chatted quite a bit, that night Raina had been out with Robert Linton.

'What did Mrs Crimmins say?' she enquired cautiously.

'That you're in need of a good husband. I gathered she was presenting Robert as a candidate.'

In spite of herself, Raina felt her cheeks burning. 'Mrs Crimmins means well,' she said.

'She's also right. About you needing a husband—and about Dan needing a father.'

'Am I doing so badly?' she asked, stung. 'You don't think much of me as a mother, do you?'

'Don't be ridiculous!' he said, keeping his voice low so that Danny shouldn't overhear. 'I've never suggested you're not a good mother. Just that you can't be a father as well. No woman can.'

'Biologically, I'll admit that's true.'

'Biologically isn't what I meant, and you know it. Stop begging the question, Raina.'

'Well, it's a fairly academic question, isn't it? I mean,

you don't seem to see Robert Linton as a suitable— proposition. Do you have a better suggestion?'

'Yes—me,' he said somewhat grimly.

Raina was so utterly surprised, she burst into a peal of laughter.

The car swerved a little as Logan took a corner, and his mouth straightened into a rather ominous line.

Fortunately, Danny created a diversion by demanding to know what had prompted her laughter, and by the time she had concocted some diplomatic reply and diverted his attention to something else, Logan's face showed nothing but a slightly grim concentration on his driving.

He was less than talkative for the rest of the trip, answering Danny's at first eager chatter with friendly brevity, and addressing only an occasional cool, impersonal comment of his own to Raina.

Danny had fallen asleep again before they reached the house, and Logan said, 'I'll take him in for you.'

He was out of the car before she could protest, lifting the sleeping child with a gentleness that belied the tight set of his mouth. Raina opened the door and he carried his slight burden into Danny's bedroom, laying him on the bed.

The child stirred, and Logan smoothed back the soft hair from the smooth forehead and said, 'Okay, son— you're home, now.'

Brown eyes flickered half open, unseeing, and the child murmured, 'Daddy—back!'

Raina stopped breathing, and Logan went very still for an instant before he straightened up and pulled the eiderdown from the bottom of the bed over the sleeping boy.

Raina turned and made blindly for the lounge, blinking back tears. She had explained as well as she could to Danny that his father had died, and would never be coming back, that he loved them and would be waiting for them to join him. She hadn't wanted to let him believe that Perry might return some day, and a year in a child's life was a long time. He might have almost forgotten that he had a father, if Raina had not made a point of keeping his memories of Perry alive with casual comments about the things they used to do together, and about things his father used to enjoy. Surely that had not been a mistake? Should she have just let him forget altogether? Because it seemed she might have been nurturing a futile hope that one day his father would come back.

She turned as Logan came into the room, standing just inside the doorway. His hands were thrust into his pockets and his eyes were keen and iceberg blue. 'Are you all right?' he asked.

'Yes, of course.' She was pale and her voice was husky, but she was perfectly composed.

'He thought I was his father.'

'Yes. He was half asleep, probably dreaming.'

Logan seemed to hesitate, an unusual thing for him. Then he said, 'I wasn't joking, you know. When I suggested you might marry me.'

Raina started a little, her heart beginning a slow pounding that seemed to threaten to suffocate her. In a strange little voice, she said, 'You can't mean it!'

'I just told you, I do.'

'I—don't understand.'

'It isn't all that difficult, surely. I'm asking you to marry me.'

'You—?' She gave a breathy, nervous little laugh.

'It's still funny?' he asked, with dangerous politeness.

'*No*, I'm sorry! It's just that—I never thought of you as a marrying man, Logan.'

'Didn't you? Well, perhaps I feel ready to settle down.'

A smile touched her mouth, with fleeting irony. The homely phrase didn't somehow fit, with Logan as its subject. 'Because Danny needs a father?' she asked him, rather gently.

He didn't move from his position near the doorway, but the hands in his pockets must have clenched, because she saw the material of his jeans tauten suddenly across the flatness of his stomach. 'It's one reason,' he said, 'for you to consider it.'

'You could never take Perry's place,' she told him, with a sudden perverse desire to shake him out of his self-control. 'For Danny—or for me.'

A muscle in his cheek flickered, tautened. 'I wouldn't try,' he said. 'I don't see myself as a stand-in for Perry.'

Raina smiled again, a little sourly. No, Logan wouldn't see himself as any sort of substitute or second best. He was always himself, first of all.

'Don't you think this is carrying your obligation to him a bit far?' she asked him.

'This has nothing to do with my promise to Perry,' he said flatly, 'and you know it.'

'Nothing——?'

He looked at her with concentration, his eyes narrowed, their gaze searingly sharp. 'This is for me,' he said. 'Not for Perry. Don't make any mistake about that. I want you—I always have. You knew it on your wedding day, and you've known it ever since. I don't care what terms you set, or what—excuses—you have to make to yourself. But *I* won't pretend to be doing this for Perry's sake—or his son's.'

Raina trembled slightly, and tightened her lips against it. 'But you don't mind if I say yes for Danny's sake?' she asked him.

'It wouldn't be such a sacrifice, Raina,' he said with soft mockery. 'I've known that since the last time I kissed you.'

'Sex,' she said scornfully. 'There's more to marriage than that.'

'It isn't such a bad basis to start with,' he said. 'Did Perry love you for your mind?'

'Leave Perry out of this!' she flashed.

'All right.' He looked oddly wary. 'I'd prefer it, actually. He does tend to—obtrude between you and me, doesn't he?'

Angrily she demanded, 'What on earth am I supposed to say to *that*?'

'Nothing. Forget I said it. As you say, we'll leave Perry out of it.'

'It might be better if we dropped the whole subject.'

'Oh, no. You haven't given me an answer.'

'Then it's no. Thank you for your flattering offer, but no.'

There was a tense silence. Logan took his hands from his pockets, and hooked his thumbs under his wide leather belt, rocking a little on his heels. 'Just like that?'

'I don't know how else to put it,' she said.

'You might give it some thought, anyway,' he suggested.

'The answer would still be no.'

'Because you still think of Perry as your husband?'

'I—yes.' Her eyes darkened, wondering at his perspicacity.

'I could change that,' he said almost violently.

'I don't *want* it changed!'

'No, you don't.' His gaze was almost hostile. 'That's

the whole trouble, isn't it? You prefer wallowing in your memories, to the challenge of life in the here and now.'

'You're being a sore loser, Logan,' she accused him.

But he said, 'I haven't lost yet. I don't give up so easily, Raina.'

After he had left, she sat down shakily on one of the soft chairs, with a strange, unsettling feeling of danger narrowly averted. Silly, she told herself. Logan had not threatened her, he had given no hint of violence except once or twice in his voice. He had offered her marriage, and been turned down. So what?

But she trembled again as she recalled his parting words. *I haven't lost yet. I don't give up . . .*

A few days later Danny developed a croaky cough, that became a whooping bark in the night, and when she went in to him, Raina found him gasping and choking for breath, his eyes filled with fear.

Frightened herself, she flew to the phone and called their doctor, and by the time he came she was almost frantic, but trying to hide it from Danny as she soothed him and encouraged him to inhale steam from a basin of hot water laced with balsam.

The doctor was a middle-aged man who diagnosed croup and gave Danny an injection, told her to continue the steam treatment and then left. He was expected somewhere else, and hadn't time to do more than check that Danny had been given his three-in-one vaccinations, and assure her that in that case he shouldn't be in any real danger.

But the rest of the dark hours were a nightmare, and it wasn't until morning that Danny fell into a real, relatively comfortable sleep.

Never had Raina wished so much for Perry's presence. She tiptoed out of Danny's room feeling limp and weak and very much alone. It would have been so much easier if only Perry had been there to share the wringing anxiety, to steady her when panic had threatened to overwhelm her, to add his voice to hers as she tried to comfort their son and assure him that he was going to be all right soon, that in the morning he would feel better . . .

She pulled her dressing gown about her waist, pushed back tangled hair and went into the kitchen to make herself a cup of tea. She drank two, trying to persuade herself to make toast, and finding the idea nauseous, one ear listening for any sound from the slightly open door of Danny's room.

The telephone bell jangled at her nerves, and she flew to answer it before it woke Danny, snatching up the receiver and breathing a cross, breathless 'Hello!' into it.

Logan's voice said, 'You were quick. I didn't get you out of bed, then?'

'I've been out of bed for hours,' she said wearily. 'What do you want?'

But he didn't answer that. His voice sharpening, he said, 'Why, what's happened?'

And she said, 'Danny——' and then choked on the tears of reaction that she couldn't hold back, unable to say anything more.

Logan said, 'Yes—Raina, *what's the matter?*'

She tried to say, 'It's all right, now,' but couldn't speak, and finally she put down the receiver and leaned against the wall, giving way to deep sobs and hiding her face in her hands.

When it was over, she tried to phone Logan back, but the rings went through with no answer. He would be on his way, of course, she thought, coming to see for himself.

She had made an utter fool of herself, breaking down

so unexpectedly. She must pull herself together before he arrived.

She pushed back her hair and made to go to her own room, and then the doorbell rang.

He couldn't have reached here already, she thought, after a stunned moment or two. She scrubbed a hand over her damp cheeks and went to see who it was.

Mrs Crimmins stood on the step, wrapped in a blue candlewick dressing gown, her face anxious.

'Mr Thorne phoned me,' she said. 'He said he thought you might need some help.'

'Oh, Mrs Crimmins, there was no need to disturb you,' Raina apologised. 'I've had a bad night with Danny, and I—I'm afraid Logan realised I was upset when he phoned, and jumped to conclusions.'

'Yes, well, come on, dear, let me in and tell me all about it,' the woman said comfortably.

Raina found herself sitting again at the kitchen table and pouring out the story of the entire night.

'You should have called me,' Mrs Crimmins clucked reprovingly. 'You shouldn't have been alone all night.'

'The doctor came—I didn't like to bother you.'

'I still say you need a good man.'

'Maybe.' Raina sighed. She had not seen Robert again, and she knew why. Logan had frightened him off. Not that she would have married Robert. She hoped Mrs Crimmins didn't intend to start matchmaking again.

'I'd better get dressed,' she said, 'before Logan arrives.'

'Yes, he said he was coming. Well, I'll be on my way, dear, unless there's anything I can do?'

'Nothing,' Raina smiled. 'Thank you, but I'll be all right once——'

'Once Mr Thorne gets here, I know,' Mrs Crimmins

said serenely. 'I don't know what you'd do without that man. Why don't you marry him? And don't tell me he hasn't asked—if he hasn't, he certainly will. He thinks a lot of you.'

Raina was relieved that the other woman seemed to expect no reply to her question. It suddenly seemed a perfectly logical question, her tired mind quite unable to find any answer, as she stripped off her limp night things and showered briefly before putting on fitting tan cord trousers and a cream blouse with a loose sleeveless jumper over it.

The pale, haggard face peering back at her from the mirror made her shudder, and she applied foundation and lipstick with a heavy hand, trying to disguise its pallor. It only made her look painted, and she scrubbed off the lipstick to start again, but had not re-applied it when Logan's imperious hand came down on the doorbell.

She sighed, and went to answer it, flinging the door open and immediately gabbling, 'There's no need for this, everything's all right, Logan!'

He stood there, his hand still just over the bell, leaning on the jamb, with the other hand on his hip, pushing back the leather jacket he wore over dark slacks and a pale blue shirt, unbuttoned at the throat.

'Thank God for that!' he said feelingly.

'I'm sorry if you were worried.'

'Sorry!' He moved suddenly, pushing her before him into the house and closing the door behind them. He looked at her keenly, his eyes sharp on her face. 'Tell me.'

She did it as briefly and unemotionally as she could, and he heard her out in silence.

Before he could comment, Danny called from the

bedroom, and she almost ran to see what he wanted, how he was.

His face was flushed and his voice strangely hoarse, but he was breathing almost normally, though his chest wheezed and whooped faintly. 'Uncle Logan,' he said. 'I want Uncle Logan.'

Logan came as Raina gave him a beckoning look over her shoulder, bending over the bed to flick the child's hot cheek, and saying, 'Well, what's all this I hear, young feller? Been getting the doctor out of his warm bed in the middle of the night, have you?'

'He gave me a prick,' Danny confided with a mixture of pride and remembered pain.

'Did he?' Logan sounded interested, even slightly impressed, and Raina saw Danny's face assume a look that he kept just for his Uncle Logan, that she thought of as his 'man-to-man' look, compounded of pride and satisfaction and—love, she supposed.

She went into the kitchen and left them together. When Logan joined her he said, 'I told him to try and get some more sleep. He's not hungry.'

Raina pushed over a cup of coffee she had just made and set on the table.

'Sit down,' she said. 'Would you like some toast—or eggs? Have you had breakfast?'

'Nothing, thanks,' he said. 'Have something yourself, you look——'

'Awful,' Raina supplied with a faint, rueful smile. 'You always seem to be telling me that. I'm surprised you want to marry me.' She paused as he lifted his cup, his eyes on the steaming liquid in it, and then she said casually, '*Do* you still want to marry me?'

Logan put down the cup without drinking from it, his blue gaze meeting hers with quick interrogation. 'I haven't changed my mind in three days,' he said levelly.

His eyes said, *Have you?* And she answered that question.

'I have,' she said. 'If the offer is still open, Logan—I'd like to accept it.'

CHAPTER FIVE

LOGAN'S expression didn't change, and for a moment she wondered if he had heard her.

Then he said slowly, 'You've had a rotten night, you're exhausted and feeling the strain of trying to manage on your own, and for once you think someone to lean on would be—nice.' He paused, then went on deliberately. 'And I'm going to take advantage of that, and hold you to what you've just said, Raina. So don't think you can go back on it, when you're feeling strong and brave and independent again.'

'I won't,' she said. 'But if I did—you could hardly force me to honour my promise, Logan.'

'Couldn't I?' he said, with warning in his eyes. 'There are ways, darling.'

He had never called her that before, and there was a sort of premeditation about it that, combined with the slight grimness of his expression, sent a shiver of belated apprehension crawling up her spine.

'You terrify me!' she said, smiling lightly, but there was more than a grain of truth in it.

A faint grin touched his mouth. 'That's proof that you're not yourself, then,' he jeered gently. 'You would never admit it otherwise.'

'Drink your coffee,' she said, uncomfortable under the scrutiny of his eyes, '—before it gets cold.'

He picked up the cup and said, 'Aren't you having any?'

'I just had two cups of tea.'

'Is that all?'

'Yes. Don't fuss, Logan. I'll get something to eat

later. It's early yet.'

As he drank the coffee, she asked, 'What did you phone so early for, anyway?'

'I thought I might take Dan out for the day,' he answered. 'And you, if you wanted to come. I was on my way to have a look at some topdressing. They're trying out a new loading machine that I want to see in action. But you won't be coming, obviously.'

'No. But thanks for the thought.'

'*You* wouldn't have come, anyway, would you?'

Raina shrugged. 'There'll be other times,' she said vaguely.

Logan put down the empty cup and said, 'That's right, there will.'

'That sounds almost like a threat,' she said challengingly.

'It was a promise,' he said, lifting his brows slightly.

An oddly strained silence fell, and she discovered that she felt strangely flat, as though they were suffering from a sort of anticlimax. She looked up and found Logan's eyes on her, a slight smile curving his mouth. She told herself that they had just become engaged, and searched his eyes for a sign of tenderness, but they seemed as cool as ever, more speculative than anything.

'What's the matter?' he asked. 'Regretting it already?'

'No. When do you want to get married?'

'Is there any need to wait? The arrangements take a couple of weeks, I think. Will that give you long enough?'

'I—I don't know. There'll be—decisions to make, won't there? And Danny will have to get used to the idea . . .'

'You mean *you* will. Dan won't be a problem.'

'How do you know that? An uncle isn't the same thing as a stepfather.'

'He can call me Uncle as long as he likes.'

Raina hesitated, her eyes down on her tightly clasped hands. Then she asked, 'Will you move in with us?'

'No,' he said uncompromisingly, 'I won't.'

'It might be better for Danny if you did . . .'

'No!' Logan repeated. 'You can't keep him wrapped in cotton wool all his life.'

'I'm not trying to!'

'All right, we won't go into that. But I don't intend to start our marriage in the house you shared with Perry.'

She couldn't reasonably expect him to, of course. She bit her lip and said, 'We can't escape the memories, Logan. Even in *your* home. Perry took me there, too.'

'I know.' Logan leaned over the table to close his hand over her knitted fingers. 'I don't want to wipe out your memories—or mine. We both—loved Perry. Maybe it's the only foundation we have to build on, except for—one that you don't want to admit.' His eyes searched hers. 'But foundations,' he told her, 'are meant to be built on, and the deeper they're buried, the stronger the building. I intend to build a strong marriage, Raina.'

Raina looked up from his imprisoning fingers on hers, with hostility in her eyes. 'You're very sure of yourself,' she said.

'Yes,' he said softly. 'And you've never liked that, have you?'

She pulled her hand away from his clasp, and said, 'I agreed to marry you because Danny loves you, and he needs a man in his life. You do realise that, don't you?'

He looked at her in silence for a moment, then said, 'I do realise why you're marrying me, Raina. I have no—illusions.'

She thought he laid faint stress on the *I* in that sentence, but his face revealed nothing.

'As long as you know,' she said stubbornly.

'Maybe I know more than you think.'

She looked away from the mockery in his eyes.

When he stood up, she glanced up at him quickly, almost with apprehension.

'I have to get moving,' he said. 'I'm expected elsewhere very shortly. I'll call back tonight to see how Dan is, and—we'll talk.'

'Yes, all right,' she said, getting to her feet to see him out. The atmosphere was strained, and she avoided his eyes as he turned in the doorway with his hand on the knob.

'Don't worry,' said Logan. 'It'll work out, Raina—I promise.'

His hand came under her chin and lifted it. His eyes scanned her face and then he lowered his head and kissed her mouth, the brief pressure of his lips hard and almost brutal, leaving a stinging warmth when he let her go and went out, closing the door behind him.

When he returned in the early evening, Danny was much better, and Raina had allowed him to get up and sit on the sofa in the lounge to watch television.

Logan received a warm but hurried greeting before Danny's attention returned to the screen. Raina shrugged apologetically and turned to go out to the kitchen, but Logan caught at her arm with strong fingers and said in a low voice, 'Have you told him?'

'No,' she admitted. 'Not yet.' His eyes were very sharp, boring into hers, and she said defensively, 'There's plenty of time. We haven't really talked, ourselves, yet.'

He nodded, and released her, but he strolled over to sit by Danny, as Raina went out to finish washing up the tea dishes and put on the electric jug to make coffee for Logan.

When she returned to the lounge, the programme had just finished, and Logan got up and switched off the set as she entered. She put the cup on a side table near the sofa, as he came to sit beside Danny again and said deliberately, 'We have something to tell you, Dan. Would you mind if I married your mother?'

Danny frowned with concentration. 'Instead of my daddy?' he asked.

Logan's smile was wry. 'Sort of,' he said. 'You see, your daddy died, so he can't look after you and your mother any more. I'd like to take over the job. Your mother has agreed, and I hope that you're going to approve of the idea.'

Danny considered. 'Mummy said people that are married look after each other, and they both look after kids,' he said. 'My mummy going to look after you, Uncle Logan?'

'I certainly hope so. But it won't stop her looking after *you*, sport. And I'll be there to help her.'

Danny looked thoughtful. 'Okay,' he said. 'That's good.'

Logan put out a large hand to gently grip the childish shoulder. 'Good lad,' he said softly. 'How would you like to come and live with me?'

'Mummy too?' Danny queried.

'Mummy too. Married people generally live together.'

'Okay,' Danny said again. 'Will you make me a swing, Uncle Logan?'

'Sure. What kind did you have in mind?' Logan asked gravely.

'A tire,' Danny explained. 'On a big rope.'

'I think I can organise that.'

After Danny had said goodnight to Logan and been packed off to bed, Raina returned to the lounge, her expression cool as she stood near the doorway, watching Logan finish his coffee and put down the empty cup.

'You had no need to do that,' she said.

'Do what?' He leaned back against the sofa and turned his head slightly to look at her.

'Burn my boats for me,' she said. 'I would have told Danny—after we talked. You were trying to make it impossible for me to change my mind, weren't you?'

'Well, if you were going to tell him anyway, what difference does it make?'

'None. Only I don't like having my hand forced, Logan.'

He shrugged. 'You know what they say—all's fair——'

She moved a little farther into the room, watching his face with curiosity. 'Which is this, Logan?' she asked. 'Love—or war?'

He stood up to face her before he answered. His gaze swept over her, amused, appreciative, frankly masculine. 'You choose,' he said.

'I don't want to fight with you, Logan. But I loved Perry, and I can't——'

'Love me?' His gaze was sardonic. 'Don't let it bother you, Raina.'

'Doesn't it bother *you*?'

'Not a lot. I'll settle for—what you *can* give me—for the moment.'

'That's very accommodating of you,' she said.

'No, it isn't. It's very pragmatic of me.'

'You're not in love with me, either,' she said. 'Are you?'

'I've told you,' he said, with a dangerous underlying violence in his voice, 'I want you. I always have.'

'*Want?*' she repeated. 'Is that all?'

'It's enough.'

'For marriage?' she almost shivered, feeling suddenly coldly afraid. 'I—don't agree.'

'Don't you?' Logan swept her with a glance of amused contempt. 'Come *here*, you little fool!'

She tried to evade him as he moved and reached for her, but he caught her wrist and pulled her into his encircling arms. She jerked her head aside, and he laughed and said, 'Don't be a prude, Raina. We're engaged, remember?'

'That doesn't give you the right——' But the rest of the words were lost as he tangled his fingers into her hair and found her lips with his mouth.

His hold on her was strong and almost cruel, but his kiss was unexpectedly gentle. His lips seemed to promise to erase her fears and doubts, to soothe her anxiety. They moved on hers, softly, at first, exploring the outline of her mouth with an intimate tenderness, until gradually her tense resistance left her, and his hold became imperceptibly less restricting, but more passionate. His hand left her hair to cradle her nape as his kiss deepened and forced her lips to part for him. His other arm brought her body close to his and she could feel the heat of his desire, and she shivered with a strange mixture of fear and triumph.

He felt it, and lifted his head for a moment to look into her eyes, his own glitteringly blue. Raina looked back with a drugged gaze, her lips still parted and moist from his kiss, and he smiled and said softly, 'Put your arms round me, Raina.'

Bewildered by her own unexpectedly aroused desire,

she shook her head and made a feeble effort at escape, but he laughed at it and captured her mouth again with his, his kiss hard now, and sure, asserting the right she had tried to deny him, telling her without words that he wouldn't allow a retraction of the response she had begun to give him.

She tried to withhold it, to remain passive in his embrace, her hands slackly at her sides. But that allowed him to hold her so intimately that she put her hands against his hard upper arms in protest. And then somehow her hands were sliding up, and holding him as he had wanted, her mouth responding to his kiss and her body trembling against his, warm and soft with a suddenly unleashed passion of her own.

Logan made an inarticulate, low sound in his throat, and then she was swung off her feet and the world seemed to be revolving in a dizzy spiral, until she felt the softness of the sofa cushions at her back, and Logan's hard maleness was pressing her down, his hands touching her throat, her breasts and hips as he caressed her, his lips trailing fire over her throat and the soft swell of her breast as he pulled the neckline of her dress away to give him access.

Her fingers touched his shoulders, and moved softly over the sinews of his neck and into his hair, feeling its crispness, and she gasped and threw back her head with a shock of pleasure as his fingers at her back drew down her zip and undid her bra, while his mouth took advantage of the fact, and intimately kissed her naked flesh.

To her half closed eyes the room seemed to be swimming in a kaleidoscopic haze, but suddenly one object in it stood out clear and stark against the rest—a photograph of Perry that stood on the bookcase in one corner. His eyes seemed to meet hers, and a wave of cold shock passed over her, so that she gasped in quite a different way, a gasp of horror and rejection, and her body shuddered in total, absolute repudiation.

Logan raised his head, and she pushed at him frantically, almost sobbing as she drew away from him, stumbling to her feet and drawing her dress about her in shame and distress.

Logan stood up, too, his face darkly flushed and his breathing harsh. 'What is it?' he demanded roughly, as she backed from him, her eyes enormous with emotion. 'For God's sake, Raina, what's the matter?'

'You—you want too much, too soon, Logan. I—I'm not ready for this.'

He stopped where he was, frowning. 'You were good and ready just a minute ago!' he said.

Raina shook her head, fumbling with the fastening of her bra, her own face hot.

More quietly, Logan said, 'I wasn't intending to get you into bed. Is that what you're afraid of?'

'I'm not afraid of anything. But I think you—you're rushing things, that's all. I think you would have taken this as far as you could, because you want—a commitment.'

'I *have* a commitment,' he reminded her. 'You've promised to marry me.'

'Yes, I have. But that doesn't seem to be enough for you. You don't trust me, do you?'

She slid the zip of her dress up from her waist as far as she could, and pushed the tumbled hair from her hot cheeks.

'What happened just now had nothing to do with my trusting you,' Logan said.

'Didn't it?' She had regained her composure, and looked at him squarely. 'I don't think I believe that, Logan.'

'You think I must always have an ulterior motive,

don't you?' he said. 'The fact is, Raina, I want to make love to you. I've wanted that for a long time, and now I'm finding it hard to wait any longer. But I have the distinct feeling that you prefer to have my ring on your finger first.'

'Is that so—strange?' she asked him.

'It depends on your reasons. When you married Perry, were you a virgin?'

Flushing wildly, she said, 'That's none of your business!'

His eyes cruelly amused, he said, 'Maybe not. It might have a bearing on our present situation, though.'

'In what possible way——?'

'It could indicate that your refusal is due to a moral scruple—and not to a simple desire to put off the inevitable for as long as you possibly can.'

Steadily she said, 'It could indicate both.'

A wry grin twisted his mouth. 'You don't give an inch if you can help it, do you, Raina? Our married life promises to be—interesting.'

His eyes raked her, with a masculine frankness that caused a strange sensation deep within her, an uncurling of a dark, secret excitement. She looked away from him, afraid of what might be in her own eyes.

'See me to the door,' said Logan.

Slightly surprised, she said, 'You're going?'

'There doesn't seem much point in staying,' he shrugged, as he stood waiting for her at the doorway of the room.

'Because I won't let you make love to me?' she asked, passing him with her head high and her eyes looking straight ahead.

He was behind her as she went down the narrow little passageway to the front entrance. 'Because you won't let me get close to you—in any way,' he answered, reaching around her to open the outer door.

His shoulder brushed hers, and she stepped away from him, her back against the wall by the door. Logan raised a hand to place it against the jamb, and put his other hand on the wall beside her, trapping her there. 'Kiss me goodnight,' he said.

Raina didn't move, and after a moment he bent his head slowly and kissed her mouth with deliberate expertise.

She didn't respond at all, and when he lifted his head there was angry frustration in his eyes. But all he said was, 'Goodnight, Raina,' before he left her and strode down the path into the darkness.

He didn't attempt to make love to her again before their wedding. She saw him almost every day, and each time he left he would drop a brief, hard kiss on her lips before leaving, but that was all.

They were married quietly on a Friday, taking only three days for an abbreviated honeymoon. Raina didn't want to leave Danny for longer than that. He was to stay with one of his friends from the play-centre whose mother had offered to have him, and then he and Raina would live in Logan's house in Hamilton.

When she removed Perry's ring from her finger on the morning of her marriage to Logan, she felt strangely frightened and guilty. She dropped the ring into a trinket box that Perry had given her on their first anniversary, and tucked the box into a corner of one of the suitcases she had packed in readiness for removal to Hamilton. The house was to be sold, its contents auctioned, and Logan had made sure she packed her personal belongings before the wedding, to be picked up immediately they returned from their three-day break.

The dress she had chosen was simply cut to emphasise her slim waist and trim figure, and the flared skirt fell in gentle folds to below her knees. The material was a soft cream chiffon printed with smoke-silver flowers, and she had found a silver lace mantilla to wear on her hair. When she walked down the aisle of the small church, and saw Logan's tall figure waiting for her, her hand trembled and she clutched desperately at the prayerbook she held, in case she should drop it. Her eyes met Logan's and found his watching her without tenderness, the ice blue gaze intent and searching, not loving at all. Blindly, she transferred her gaze to the altar before them, and didn't look at him again. His responses were firm and sure, and hers were low and hesitant. She was possessed by a feeling of dread, and when his hand placed the ring on her finger, covering the place where Perry's ring had been, her fingers shook uncontrollably until Logan's closed over them in a grip that hurt.

She signed the register with a sudden piercing knowledge that this was the last time she would use Perry's name. And when she looked up she found Logan's eyes on her, and a vivid memory of her first wedding day made her eyes suddenly darken. She remembered Logan's lips on hers, while Perry's hand rested lightly on her waist. This time there was no best man or bridesmaid, only Mrs Crimmins and one of Logan's engineers who had acted as the official witnesses. This time Logan didn't kiss her, and she was thankful for that.

Danny had sat through the ceremony beside Mrs Crimmins, religiously solemn and good, and as the minister ushered the official party down the altar steps, Raina's heart turned over with love at the sight of his eager face, his eyes shining with the importance of the occasion.

He looked at them and asked in a piercing whisper, 'Are you married now?'

'We sure are, sport,' Logan grinned, and stooped to swing the child up in one arm, so that the three of them went down the aisle and out of the church together. Mrs Crimmins smiled, wiped away a sentimental tear and pulled a pocket camera from her capacious handbag to record the occasion, making them pause at the church entrance while she happily snapped several pictures.

Afterwards, with the few friends they had invited to be present, they had a champagne breakfast at a nearby hotel restaurant. Raina ate little, feeling more and more strung up as the meal wore on and everyone except Logan and she became gay and convivial.

In an effort to lift her spirits, Raina drank more champagne than she was accustomed to, and found that the effect was to blur everything a little. But when she caught Logan's gaze it was sharply in focus, and his expression was hard and brooding.

He had booked a room for them to change in, and she was relieved when he suggested that they should get ready to leave.

Her vision swam as she stood up, and she was glad of Logan's steadying hand on her arm. He almost pushed her up the stairs and into the room, closing the door behind them before he released her arm, so suddenly that she nearly stumbled.

Her overnight bag was on the bed, and she crossed the room on unsteady legs to open it and shake out the shirt and linen-look skirt she had packed in it the night before. She was very aware that Logan was watching her, leaning against the door with his arms folded, and a sardonic twist to his mouth.

She laid the clothes on the bed and took out a small vanity bag. Her fingers trembled and as she turned from the bed, the bag slipped and fell to the carpeted floor with a soft thud.

She stooped hastily to retrieve it, swaying a little as she straightened again with the bag firmly clutched, this time, in her hand. Logan still leaned on the door, and the curve of his mouth was almost a sneer, so that she asked sharply, 'Why are you looking at me like that?'

'I'm your husband,' he said. 'Doesn't that give me the right to look at you?'

Her husband. She didn't feel that he was her husband. It didn't seem as though he was enjoying the thought, either. And she didn't like the way he looked at her. 'What's so funny?' she challenged him, because he seemed to be finding something funny, in a bitter sort of way.

'You,' he said. 'Is marrying me such an ordeal that you can only bear it through an alcoholic haze?'

Furiously, she said, 'I'm not drunk!'

'You're damned close to it,' he said brutally. 'You can hardly walk straight.'

She jerked her gaze away from him, the movement making her head swim rather alarmingly. 'Do you mind if I have the bathroom first?' she asked him coldly.

'Not at all. Take your time—cold water might do the trick.'

She flashed him as chilly a glance as she could muster, and made for the bathroom door.

When she came out, he had discarded his jacket and tie, and was standing by the window, looking out. He turned and glanced at her, but she wouldn't look at him, and after a moment he took some things from a small case standing on the floor and went into the bathroom.

Raina changed her clothes hastily, and was combing her hair before the dressing table mirror when Logan returned. He had stripped to his brief dark underpants, and she averted her eyes from the broad tanned chest and hair-darkened long legs and went on combing as he pulled on casual sand-coloured pants and a tan shirt.

He asked, 'Would you like to say goodbye to Dan here—alone?'

'Yes,' she said. 'Thank you.'

'I'll fetch him.'

He had his hand on the door knob when she said, 'Logan——?'

'Yes?'

Her head was bent, her eyes on the blue comb she held in her hand. 'Try to understand—this isn't the first time for me, and—I keep remembering how it was—with Perry. I'm sorry if—it hasn't been the wedding day you hoped for. It—isn't easy for either of us.'

He didn't answer for several moments. Then he said, 'Well, it isn't over yet, is it? I'll get Dan.'

Danny was very casual about her 'little holiday with Uncle Logan' and seemed impatient to see her off, so that she was torn between relief and chagrin. With Mrs Crimmins by his side, he waved to them cheerfully as Logan drove them away from the hotel. Settling back in her seat and fastening her safety belt, Raina said, 'He seems quite happy about it all.'

'He is,' said Logan. 'I told you there wouldn't be a problem there.'

She hadn't asked where they were going. She had told Logan she had no preference, and would leave the choice to him. He knew that she and Perry had spent their honeymoon in the famous thermal district of Rotorua with its hot pools and geysers, and she was sure that Logan would not take her there.

They headed south, and were soon passing through

the pretty tree-lined streets of Cambridge, then driving on through rolling country interspersed with stands of willow and poplar as well as the odd pocket of dark native bush. The road ran alongside the great Waikato river for a time, and they passed a signpost pointing the way to the Karapiro dam where hydro-electricity was produced from the roaring volume of water that passed over it each day. At Tirau, a small thriving township built on a hill, Raina was relieved when Logan ignored the Rotorua turn-off and took the main highway towards Lake Taupo, the North Island's inland sea.

Some time later they stopped for a snack at the timber town of Tokoroa before entering the great Kinleith forest with its brooding pines lining the roadside and covering the hillsides. At Wairakei they stopped to stare curiously at the maze of pipes and machinery installed in the seething valley to tap the underground power released by natural steam bores. These filled the valley with hissing white clouds, and rumbled beneath their feet as they stood on the barren ground where the heat, sulphur and steam discouraged plant growth. And late in the afternoon they drove into Taupo and down its wide main street to the lake shore, which they followed for a further few miles to a secluded bay.

A clean little cottage awaited them, tucked away out of sight under some trees, just a few yards from the gently lapping waters of the lake and away from the road, so that the first thing Raina noticed when Logan stopped the car engine, was the complete quietness of the place.

After they had unpacked, and investigated the cupboards that had been stocked for them, and made a meal of steak and salad which they ate almost in silence, they strolled outside. The stars were pricking the sky with pinpoints of light, pale gold against deepening indigo, and the lake was misty and mysterious in the dusk. The waves licked softly at the narrow shoreline with a soft, insistent rippling sound, and birds chirped sleepy goodnights to each other from tree to tree. An evening breeze rustled the leaves overhead, and at their feet a cricket sang an intermittent song.

A movement on the lake and a plop made Logan grip Raina's arm and point. It happened again, and she saw the curved silver body of a trout leap from the water, momentarily gleaming in the last light of the day before it disappeared, leaving a ring of ripples behind.

'Do you fancy fishing?' Logan asked quietly.

Raina shook her head. 'Do you?'

'Not at the moment. I have other things in mind for the next few days.'

She didn't answer, or look at him, her eyes on the white sand before them as she went on walking at the water's edge, the breeze catching at her hair and her skirt. It freshened, and she rubbed her hands over her upper arms as goose pimples began to rise on them.

'Are you cold?' asked Logan, his arm coming about her shoulders, his warm hand caressing her arm.

'A bit.' She stopped walking as the pressure of his hand increased, and he turned her in his arms. He held her lightly, looking down at her face in the dimness, his eyes questioning.

She had no answer for him, and her own eyes fell, lighting on the open collar of his shirt, and watching with fascination the hurried beating of a pulse in the hollow of his tanned throat.

'Raina——' he said.

His arms tightened a little. Raina moistened her lips with her tongue, and lifted a hand slowly, until her finger was on that beating pulse. She touched it and felt its tiny rhythmic movement against her finger.

Then he said her name again, and his hand grabbed at hers and carried it to his mouth. He closed his mouth over her finger, then moved his lips down to her palm and her wrist.

Raina drew a sharp breath of pleasure, and he lifted his mouth from her wrist and looked at her again, his eyes searing her in the growing darkness. His feet shifted, and one of his hands ran down her back, pulling her close to him, until her thighs were pressed against his. His other arm curved about her shoulders, and his mouth came down over hers, pressing her head back against his arm, opening her lips with a ruthless passion. The stars danced behind her closed eyelids, the gentle hiss of the waves receded before the rushing sound in her ears, and the cool night air had no power to chill against the heat of desire that coursed through her from head to toe. Her hands clung to him, the only stable thing in her madly spinning universe, and his hand was intimately moving on her body, awaking long-dormant responses, evoking tiny, soft sounds of delight from her against his invading mouth.

When he reluctantly loosened his hold, she was trembling again, but not with cold. He said, 'Let's go in,' and she whispered, 'Yes.'

Her legs were weak, and after the first few steps he swung her up into his arms and carried her to the open door of the cottage.

He kicked the door shut with his foot, and crossed the floor to the bedroom. There were no lights on, and in the darkness he laid her on the bed and kissed her with increasing passion. Her hands were on his shoulders, glorying in the latent muscular strength of them, and her body was singing under the weight of his.

When he moved she made a protesting attempt to hold him, and he laughed softly, triumphantly. She heard his shoes hit the mat on the floor, then felt his hands removing her sandals from her feet, and his lips fleetingly caressed the arch of one foot and then the other.

He sat on the side of the bed and pulled off his shirt, then leaned over to bring her up beside him and across his body while he kissed her again. His fingers unfastened the buttons of her blouse, and his mouth moved down her throat to her shoulders as he eased the fabric off them. He found the fastening of her bra and freed her breasts, and his palms closed over them as he laid her gently back against the pillows again.

Raina closed her eyes and her lips parted in silent ecstasy. When Logan's hands slid to her back she arched her body against his, and in her ear his voice muttered deeply, 'Beautiful—you're so beautiful—and I've wanted this for so long. Since that first time I kissed you—and you've wanted it too, haven't you——?'

The slow fire that had been consuming her was suddenly doused. She whispered hoarsely, 'No——!' And her head twisted frantically away from his kiss as he caught her mouth again with his. *'No!'* she repeated. 'I never wanted you, Logan! Only Perry——'

He stopped her movement away from him, his hands hard on her arms. 'Okay, okay,' he said, 'I shouldn't have said it. Forget it.'

She moved her head from side to side in distress, in negation, and he repeated, 'Forget it. You want me *now*. That's all that matters.'

But she couldn't forget it. As his caresses became more urgent, and his kisses bruised her lips, she felt her body grow cold and rigid, and Logan felt it, too. She knew that he checked his passion deliberately, and tried to patiently make up for what had happened, to start over again and take her slowly back to the peak of desire she had reached before. But there was a hardness inside her that refused to be melted, and her old antagonism had returned, so that she took a vicious satisfaction in her own lack of pleasure, in knowing that whatever he did, however he caressed her, her body lacked any response for him.

But Logan's body would not be denied its own desire. In the end, he stopped trying to control it. He took her in anger, and she endured it in hatred and resentment, and afterwards lay in bitter silence while he cursed her, then left her lying dry-eyed in the darkness. She heard the rustling of his clothes as he fumbled them on, and then the sound of the outer door being opened and slammed shut. He didn't come back for hours. At dawn she heard the door quietly open again, but he didn't come into the room, and shortly afterwards, she drifted at last off to sleep.

CHAPTER SIX

WHEN Raina woke it was fully light, and she peered at her watch to find that the time was after nine.

The cottage was very quiet, and when she looked out into the living room, it was empty. The cushions on the divan near the window were dented and the cotton cover rumpled, and she deduced that Logan might have spent a few uncomfortable hours there before going out again.

She showered in the compact little bathroom and dressed in a knitted cotton shirt and fitting denim trousers. In the kitchen there was no evidence that Logan had eaten, and she made toast and bacon and eggs, turning the eggs on to plates just as Logan appeared in the doorway of the kitchen.

He stood watching her with no expression on his dark face. He had shaved and was dressed in the casual pants he had worn the day before, but his shirt was white, accentuating his tan and his nearly black hair.

Composedly, Raina said, 'Good morning.'

'Good morning,' he answered, coming into the room. 'Can I help?'

'It's all done,' she said crisply. 'You do like bacon and eggs, don't you?'

He seemed to hesitate before he said, 'Yes. Thank you.'

She put the two plates on the table, with a pile of toast between them, and sat down. Logan stood at the other side, then slowly pulled out a chair for himself. He sat with his hands curled into fists clenched at either side of his plate, and Raina took a piece of toast and began unconcernedly buttering it, not looking up at all.

She cut the toast and began eating, but it was several minutes before Logan picked up his knife and fork and followed suit.

Raina said, 'Is it a nice day outside?'

'Yes,' he said briefly.

'Did you swim?'

'Yes. And the water's fine. Let's cut out the small-talk, shall we?'

'All right.' Raina pushed away her plate and got up to plug in the electric jug. 'Would you like tea or coffee?'

His fork clattered on to the plate before him. 'Either. Raina—last night——'

Raina rattled two cups into their saucers. 'Coffee,' she said. 'Do you want sugar?'

'You know perfectly well how I like my coffee,' Logan said roughly. He pushed back his chair and stood up, coming to stand behind her as she spooned instant coffee into the cups. As she put down the spoon he caught her arm, turning her to face him.

Raina jerked her arm out of his grasp and backed away. *'Don't touch me!'* she exclaimed fiercely.

Violence looked out of his eyes, and his mouth tightened, but he didn't attempt to touch her again. He said, 'Raina, that fiasco last night was my fault. I was a fool—and then a brute.'

'Well, you can't help what you are,' she said with false lightness, and was glad to see a dark colour on his cheekbones.

'I'm trying to apologise,' he said grittily.

'Do you think an *apology* will make it all right?' she asked witheringly.

'No. But I think one is—necessary. There's only one way to make it all right.'

She knew what he meant, and shook her head in rejection. 'No,' she said clearly.

'You've got to give our marriage a chance!' he said, and she knew the violence was still in him, although he was trying to suppress it.

'You mean I have to allow you your marital rights?' she taunted him. 'All right Logan, I won't deny you that. On last night's showing, it wouldn't do me much good if I tried . . . You can be pretty ruthless when you want something, can't you? You *wanted me*, you said—and now you've got me, for better or worse . . . You said you didn't care if I married you for Danny's sake, or any other reason, so long as I did marry you. Well, I did it for Danny, Logan. You'd better remember that. I would do anything for Perry's son!'

'Don't fool yourself, Raina! You didn't sacrifice yourself for Dan. You responded to me—even last night, until I said the wrong thing—you've wanted me to make love to you.'

'Not *you*, Logan,' she said coolly. 'Any man would have done, for *that*. Any reasonably attractive man with a practised technique like yours. I'm a woman—a woman who has known love—and lovemaking. I—missed it, and yes, you turned me on. That's all it was, and it was apparently enough for you. I never pretended I could give you what I gave to Perry—and you never asked for my love. And you're good for Danny. Danny needs you, and that's why I will go along with anything you demand of me, Logan. But don't expect me to put you in Perry's place. I loved him, and I'll always love his memory. You can *never* be to me what he was!'

There was a white tautness about his mouth, and his eyes were chips of ice. 'I wouldn't want to be,' he said. 'Keep your pretty memories. Keep Perry in your heart if you want to. *I'll* be the one who's in your—bed.'

Shaken, she said in a low voice, 'You really *are* a brute!'

'Thanks. Would you like me to prove it?' His eyes were merciless, making his meaning unmistakable.

Raina whitened, instinctively pressing against the counter behind her. 'I told you, I won't—deny you,' she whispered through stiff lips.

'And you'll close your eyes and think of Perry,' he jeered. 'Do you think you can keep up the iceberg act, Raina?'

He reached for her and jerked her close to him, and she stayed passive in his arms, her eyes looking past his shoulder. His hand took her chin and made her look at him. He inspected the cold defiance in her eyes, and his mouth twisted. 'Well, I won't put it to the test,' he said softly. 'I've never cared for three in a bed.'

He released her suddenly and turned on his heel, leaving her clutching at the counter for support as she heard him close the outer door behind him.

It was an odd sort of honeymoon. Logan took a spare blanket from the bedroom and slept on the divan in the living room for the next two nights, and in the morning after breakfast he went out. There was a boat kept under a lean-to by the lake, and he spent a lot of time out in it, rowing strongly and ignoring the outboard motor that was fixed to the stern. Once he asked Raina if she wanted to come, and she declined. They spoke to each other like polite strangers, and only seldom. Raina spent the days walking alone along the lake shore, or sun-bathing in a sheltered little spot on the sand under a bank which kept the breezes at bay.

On Monday morning they left quite early. There didn't seem any reason to stay, and Raina was relieved more than anything else, when Logan suggested in clipped tones that if they left soon after breakfast they could be home in plenty of time to collect her things from the house and pick up Dan.

When they reached Te Ahu and he drew up outside the house, she experienced an odd reluctance to go in. Logan got out of the car and opened her door, and she fumbled in her bag to find the key as they walked up the concrete path.

He took the key from her hand and opened the door, stepping back to let her go in ahead of him.

The emptiness was tangible, as though the place had been untenanted for much longer than three days. In the bedroom the suitcases she had packed stood on the carpet at the foot of the bed, and an air of sadness seemed to pervade the room.

Logan picked up the cases without a word and took them out, and Raina lingered, her gaze on the bed she had shared with Perry, going to the curtains that she had made herself when they first bought the house, the patch on the wallpaper where she had removed the picture they had chosen together on their honeymoon.

Logan came back to find her, and saw the tears trembling on her lashes. He stood in the doorway, saying nothing, his face a mask that might have been carved in stone. Then he turned and went out again without a word.

She joined him in the car ten minutes later, and he started the engine and drove in silence to the house where Danny was staying.

Danny helped to ease the tension on the way to Logan's house in Hamilton. He was full of what he had done over the weekend, and his chatter disguised the silence between the two grown-ups.

Logan's house was a gracious old villa overlooking the river that wound its way through the city. An old oak and an enormous rhododendron with cerise flowers dominated the front lawn, and at the back the ground sloped gently and then took a sharp dip to the water. A new high fence cut off the grounds from the river, to keep Danny safe, but the bedrooms still looked over the water.

Danny had already seen the room which was to be his, and he darted off as soon as the door was opened to establish his claim. Logan carried his own bag and some of Raina's to the main bedroom, and she followed him slowly.

She had not been in this room before. There was a wide bed covered in tobacco brown heavy silk, and a thick white rug on the floor. As she hesitated in the doorway, Logan turned from putting the cases on the floor and looked at her. 'Won't Dan expect us to share a room?' he asked.

'I don't know. I—suppose so.'

'You want him to think we're happily married, don't you? Like the people in his story books.'

'Yes. Logan, we could be more——'

'Close?' he suggested, as she hesitated, groping for words. 'That's up to you.'

'There's more to life—even married life—than sex,' she said, with a flash of anger.

'Don't I know it?' He seemed amused at her anger. 'There are more ways of being close, too.'

Danny erupted down the passageway then, calling her to come and see his room again, demanding that she help him unpack and put away his things. Until he went to bed, there would be no chance for any more private talk with Logan.

It was late before Danny was settled, excitement keeping him bright-eyed and wide awake until well past his usual bedtime. It was strange to be sitting in Logan's big lounge alone with him, strange to know that his home was now hers. Her eyes roamed about the room, lingering on the big kauri dresser in one corner, its age and ornate carving accentuated by and yet complementing the modern chairs in mahogany and dark brown leather, and the wide square coffee table placed on an oriental rug. Perry had laughed at Logan when he chose this house, and again when he had bought the kauri dresser, accused him teasingly of over-compensating for his lack of roots and background by ensconcing himself among relics of the past. From anyone else it might have been cruel, but Perry shared Logan's background, or lack of it, and Logan had merely grinned and said he preferred to live in an older house because it had more room than any of the modern boxes he had seen; and had bought the Victorian dresser because a modern cocktail cabinet would have been out of place in the house.

Logan got up now and went to open the carved door of the cupboard. 'Would you like a nightcap?' he asked Raina.

'Thank you,' she said, and he poured brandy for them both and handed her one.

The night was warm, and the big grate remained empty, but they sat in chairs at either side of it, and the effect should have been cosy. It wasn't, and as Raina swirled the dark liquid and sipped at it, she felt Logan's gaze like a lick of flame, and her nerves tensed.

Logan looked relaxed; she didn't raise her eyes as far as his face, but he leaned back comfortably in the big chair, his long legs stretched before him, and one hand lying on the arm of the chair, the fingers loose against the leather.

Raina finished her drink, and he got up and took her glass. 'Another?'

'No, thank you. I'm tired. I think I'll go to bed.'

Logan put the two glasses down on the mantelpiece and said, 'Are you really tired, or are you afraid of being alone with me?'

'I've been alone with you for three days.'

'Yes. But you didn't seem as nervous as you are now.'

'I'm not nervous.'

He bent to her and pulled her up, his hand on her slim wrist. His fingers touched her pulse, and he said mockingly, 'I'm sure it's faster than it should be. Is it fear or excitement?'

'I'm not afraid of you, and you don't excite me,' she said with contempt. 'Let me go, Logan.'

She made a tentative movement of her wrist, but when his fingers tightened she stayed still in his grasp, her eyes meeting the angry light in his with a blank indifference.

'Maybe I can change that,' he said.

'By hurting me?'

'*Am* I hurting you?'

'You would—if I fought you.'

'But you said you wouldn't fight me, didn't you, Raina? If I wanted to assert my—rights.'

His thumb moved on her inner wrist, sensuously, and she curled her fingers tightly to hide a sudden tremor. 'I won't fight you,' she whispered, her eyes held by his.

His hand went to her waist, and pulled her quite slowly closer to him. He released her wrist, and she let it drop by her side, perfectly passive in his arms, allowing him to take her face in his hand and turn it up for his kiss.

His mouth was warm and hard and searching, demanding the response which she refused to give. His hand wandered from her cheek to her throat and lingered there, his thumb pressing gently on the small hollow at its base as he bent her head back under his deepening kiss. His hand moved farther down and cupped the firm curve of her breast, and with his thumb began a tantalising stroking movement, back and forth.

Her hands clenched but remained hanging by her sides, and though her mouth was forced open under his, she would not return his kiss. But a slow trickle of sensation warmed her stomach and thighs, and when he moved his hands to force her hips against his, she wrenched her mouth away with a husky little cry of protest.

'What's the matter?' he asked. His hands moved slowly up her back, stroking it, then he drew the back of his fingers down her averted cheek. 'Was that fear?' he taunted gently. 'Or excitement?'

Raina bit her lip fiercely, and his fingers turned her face to his again. He touched her lips with his in a fleeting kiss, and then she was free, so suddenly that she almost lost her balance.

'Goodnight, Raina,' he said.

She turned from him uncertainly, unable to echo his calm goodnight, and went out of the room on shaking legs. She wasn't sure if he had believed her lack of response was genuine, or if he was playing some cat-and-mouse game of his own.

Feeling strangely unsettled, she used the bathroom, undressed slowly and climbed into the big bed. Turning out the light, she lay tensely staring into the darkness. Logan came in some time later, and she closed her eyes and tried to breathe evenly. He moved about in the darkness quietly, and then she knew that he was standing by the bed, looking down at her. Her muscles tightened, but with an effort she remained still.

He said, mockery lacing his voice, 'I've already got

the message, Raina. There's no need to pretend to be asleep. I'll be sleeping in the spare room.'

She held her breath until he had gone, and when the door closed softly behind him, she felt a strong, urgent wish to hurl something heavy after him. She was awake and restless for a long time.

Danny settled into his new home as though he had always belonged there. Logan made him a swing, and then with Danny's enthusiastic if inexpert help, built a tree hut in a fork of the big oak on the front lawn. The two of them spent a lot of time together when Logan was home, and Raina found herself stifling an odd kind of jealousy. Danny and she had been so close, and now she sometimes felt that Logan was taking her son from her. She would stand concealed by the curtains behind one of the windows, and watch as Logan taught the boy how to drive a nail or saw a plank, his big hand on Danny's small shoulder, or his dark head close to Danny's soft, flushed cheek. And she would feel a hard aching in her throat, and her fingers curling into her palms until her nails made marks on the skin.

When Logan gave the child one of his lazy grins, and Danny's face turned up to his with hero-worship in his eyes, it was all she could do not to run to her son and snatch him away. She felt trapped and confused and desperately unhappy. And Logan's attitude to her didn't help.

He would come home each day and with a hard hand under her chin, press an equally hard kiss on her soft mouth, and she could not avoid that because Danny was nearly always there, and before him she would allow no hint of friction to be seen. And Logan knew it. The tightness of his smile when he said softly, 'Hello, Raina,' the mockery in his voice, underlined his knowledge and dared her to complain. He would spend the time until she served their dinner with Danny, and afterwards he washed up while she got Danny ready for bed. On the surface it was a very normal marriage and Logan was a good substitute father. But there was always the underlying tension between Logan and herself, made more intense by her consciousness that he watched her all the time like a man waiting for something— something that would bring the situation to a head.

Raina would sit watching television or reading, knowing that his cool eyes were on her face, and he didn't bother to look away if her own eyes met them. Nor would his expression change. And eventually it was she who would wrench her gaze away and pretend to return her attention to the images on the screen or the pages of her book. She was relieved on the evenings when Logan shut himself in the small room he used as a study, and was immersed in paper work.

Every night she went to bed alone, and although his clothes remained in the room she occupied, and he sometimes walked in unannounced, his mouth curling faintly if he found her in the act of dressing or undressing, he continued to sleep in the spare room.

Raina felt that they were living in a sort of hiatus. It couldn't possibly last, and she was afraid of how it might end.

She took Danny to a nearby play-centre twice a week, and he had begun to make new friends. One of them invited him over one day after the session and, having checked that the friend's mother approved, Raina agreed to let him go. She promised to pick him up at five.

It meant she had the afternoon free, and instead of going home to the big, empty house, to be alone with her thoughts, she bought herself some sandwiches and went to the tranquil lake almost in the centre of the city, and sat idly throwing crusts to the greedy ducks and graceful swans between bites. A young couple and their toddler strolled along the shore, and the child gleefully chased after the ducks on unsteady legs, while the laughter of his parents floated back to her. Raina watched as the man took the young woman's hand in his, and she smiled at him and nuzzled her fair head against his shoulder, before she broke away to scoop their son away from the edge of the water. He came up to her and took the child from her arms, and for a moment their three heads were close together, and Raina had a sudden clear mental picture of Danny and Logan with their heads close like that, smiling at each other, and herself standing apart, aloof and lonely.

She got up, screwing up the white paper bag in her hand, brushing crumbs from her skirt, and tossed the balled paper into a wastebin. Then she walked briskly to the little car which she and Perry had bought, but Perry was not the man in her thoughts now.

There was plenty of time to drive out to the airfield and see Logan before she had to pick up Danny. She didn't rehearse what she wanted to say, and though tremors of nervousness made her bite her lip and tighten her hands on the wheel now and then, she drove steadily and with purpose. They couldn't go on like this, and it was up to her to make the first move. For Danny's sake, their marriage had to be some sort of genuine relationship. She would show Logan that she was willing to make a go of it, and surely he would meet her half-way?

She parked behind the office, and anxiously checked her appearance in the tiny rear-vision mirror. She was pale, and her eyes looked luminous and apprehensive, and when she applied some colour to her lips her fingers shook. But her cream silk blouse looked fresh and cool with the blue skirt and navy high-heeled shoes, and she didn't look nearly as nervous as she felt.

When she walked into the outer office, there was no one sitting in the orange typist's chair behind the desk, and the electric typewriter was silent.

From behind the frosted glass door of the inner office came a murmur of voices, and as she hesitated a figure appeared and she could see the blonde halo of the girl Angela's head, and a blur of something pink that she was wearing.

Raina took a step forward, ready to go in if the girl was leaving the office now, and then she heard Angela say something in a slightly raised but muffled voice, then another figure appeared, big and dark and bulky, and a small sound of protest escaped her throat as the two figures behind the glass suddenly merged into one, two heads, the dark and the fair, so close that they became indistinguishable, and the dark bar of Logan's sleeve crossing the pink blur as he put his arms about the girl.

Raina, her eyes fixed disbelievingly on the indistinct but so graphic picture, backed instinctively, and then, her skin crawling with nameless emotions, very quietly went out.

The car was a haven, and she climbed into it and fumbled the key into the ignition, trying to keep her mind quite blank, but unable to blot out the blurred image of two people locked together in an embrace. She ground the gears, swore softly and savagely sank her teeth into her lower lip as she started again, and spun the wheel to get out of the little car-park. The roar of a plane coming in to land drowned the engine noise of the car as she speeded out of the gate, pushing down the accelerator hard so that in minutes she was over the speed limit.

The green paddocks flew by, and curious cows hung over the barbed wire fences watching the car hurtle past, but it wasn't until a siren wailed in her ear that Raina realised how fast she had been driving. She had only felt an urgent need to get away as quickly and as far as she could.

The traffic officer was unimpressed by her frank admission that she had been thinking of something else, and as he imperturbably wrote out a traffic offence notice he advised her to keep her mind on her driving in future.

'Yes, Officer, I'm sorry,' she murmured automatically, taking the ominous little slip that he handed to her. He nodded to her, adjusted his cap and strode back to his own car. Raina sat in hers for some time after he had driven away and she had thrust the paper into the glove box. She felt as though she had received a body blow from which she had not recovered. It was an effort to start the car again and get going at a more sedate pace towards Hamilton.

It was too early to pick up Danny, and she parked the car in the garage and went on leaden feet into the house. The telephone was ringing, and she answered it automatically. It was the mother of Danny's friend, and she said the boys were getting along terrifically well, and could Danny please stay overnight.

'Yes,' said Raina, 'that would be nice. Thank you, I'll bring his pyjamas and toothbrush over.'

Yesterday she would have demurred, wondering if Danny would be all right—she didn't really know the woman very well, although her son was a nice polite little boy. But today she was relieved that Danny would not be here tonight. Because tonight she didn't think she would be able to retain a semblance of normality when Logan came home. And she didn't want Danny to be worried.

She packed a change of clothing and some pyjamas

and Danny's toothbrush into a duffle bag, and took them out to the car. When she got to the place, it was a pleasant suburban home, and the friend's mother said, 'Come in and have a cup of tea. I'm Sally, by the way. I never caught your name?'

'Raina.'

'That's pretty—and so unusual. Come in, Raina—the boys are about somewhere——'

They were, and so absorbed in their play that Danny scarcely seemed to notice Raina was there. She had tea with Sally and chatted, and was surprised because she was still functioning so normally, and the cold numbness inside her didn't stop her from drinking tea and smiling and telling Sally that no, she didn't think Danny would wet the bed, and he loved cornflakes for breakfast. Sally's nice suburban husband came home, and she smiled at him, too, and wondered if he had a secretary and if she was pretty and if he ever made love to her while Sally was looking after his child . . .

By the time she got home it was getting late, and she had only just gone into the kitchen, and automatically taken some potatoes out of the cupboard to peel, when she heard Logan's car.

When he came into the kitchen she was standing with her back to the door, peeling potatoes at the sink. She knew the moment when he came in and saw her, and the knife slipped and a tiny trickle of blood ran down her finger.

Logan asked, 'Where's Danny?'

Raina put her finger under the cold tap and said, 'He's staying with a friend.'

'What have you done?' He came over to stand beside her and she turned off the tap and said, without looking at him, 'It's nothing. I'll get a plaster——'

She made to turn away to get the first aid kit in

one of the cupboards.

'Let's see,' said Logan, and took her hand, stopping her.

And Raina, without thinking, acting on blind, instinctive rage, hissed, *'Don't touch me!'* and raised her other wet hand to bring the back of it sharply across his face.

She backed away from the stunned look of fury on his face, the blaze of retribution in his eyes. She was appalled by what she had done, but curiously elated, too. She had wanted to do something violent to him, to punish him in the most primitive way, and she had done it. He could do much worse to her, of course, if he had a mind to it, and he certainly looked capable of murder, but she had got in the first blow. There was satisfaction in that.

But he didn't retaliate. Instead he suddenly turned and left her without a word or another glance. She watched him go, then found the first aid box and clumsily got out a plaster dressing and fastened it about her finger.

She forgot to salt the potatoes and the steak was slightly underdone, but she served a creditable meal, gently determined that she wasn't going to go to pieces. A tiny voice inside her whispered that it was no wonder Logan had turned to another woman for comfort, for—loving, since she herself had rejected him. But they had been married less than a month, and she had gone to him today to offer to start again, to try and make things come right. And surely he could have waited a little longer, been a bit more patient, at least made some effort to understand?

Had he ever *meant* to be faithful? she wondered bitterly. He had never shown signs of being a one-woman man before, and perhaps she had been naïve in thinking that marriage meant fidelity, to him. Perry used to speak of Logan's ability to attract women with admiration and even, sometimes, a note of envy in his voice.

They ate the meal in chilly silence. Raina almost choked on hers, but somehow managed to get most of it down. When she brought in coffee, Logan pushed back his chair a little and watched her as she sat down again and raised her cup to her lips. His hand lay on the table close to his own cup.

Raina sipped nervously, aware of the rather frightening glitter in his eyes and trying to ignore it.

She finished her drink and put down the cup, the small clatter it made as it touched the saucer sounding abnormally loud in the silence. She said, 'Aren't you going to drink your coffee?'

After a moment, Logan said, 'Sure.' He hadn't taken his eyes off her, and she moved restlessly under the disconcerting scrutiny, fiddling with her empty cup, picking up her spoon and replacing it in the saucer. When at last Logan lifted his cup and drained it, she jumped up as though released from a spell, and began clearing the table.

Logan put down his cup and said curtly, 'I'll do it.'

'Danny isn't here,' she said. 'I can——'

'I *said*, I'll do it!'

'All right,' she said, tight-lipped. 'Thank you.'

She left him and went into the lounge to switch on the television, but she hardly took in the news report or the comedy which followed it. She heard Logan's chair scrape back in the dining room, the clatter of dishes, his movements in the kitchen as he washed up.

There weren't many dishes, just for the two of them, but it was a long time before he came into the lounge and sat down in a chair near hers. Resolutely, Raina glued her gaze to the screen, as though absorbed in the programme. Logan had the paper in his hand, but he didn't open it.

When the advertisements came on, the silence between them seemed louder than the enthusiastic chatter on the screen, and to break it she asked desperately, 'Did you have a good day?'

He said deliberately, 'Actually, I've had a lousy day.'

Why? she wondered. Was Angela being difficult about his marriage?

He enquired, 'How was yours?' with such politeness that she knew he was being sarcastic.

'So-so,' she shrugged.

'What did you do?'

She stiffened, casting him a wary glance. But he didn't know—he couldn't. She said, 'I took Danny to play-centre—I was on duty today, so I stayed there for the morning. Had lunch by the lake, and then spent the afternoon with Sally French—that's who Danny's staying with tonight.'

'Do I know her?'

'No. I hardly know her myself. I've seen her at the centre, but we never really talked until today.'

'But you let Danny stay the night?'

Sensing criticism, she flashed, 'He's *my* son, Logan! I'll decide who he stays with, thank you!'

Logan stood up, and she inwardly cringed. He looked very big when he stood so close, and she knew very well his temper had been simmering all evening.

'I thought we'd decided to share his upbringing,' he said, his voice quite even.

'You don't want to share!' she said bitterly, and got to her feet, too. He was still taller, but it left her at less of a disadvantage than before. 'You want to take over!' she accused him. 'Well, I won't let you! Danny's my son and Perry's, not yours!'

His jaw tightened ominously. 'As you're still Perry's wife?' he said, quite softly, but the undertone of menace sent a shiver crawling up her spine.

'If you like!' she cried recklessly.

'No,' he said, 'I don't like—I don't like it at all, and I won't have it, Raina! Not any longer. Perry's dead, and you're *my* wife, whether you're willing to accept it or not. And you had better accept it, darling, because I've had it up to *here* with playing Sir Galahad while you sort yourself out. I don't take kindly to having my face slapped when I touch my own wife. It won't happen again—understand?'

Fear and fury burst into action, and she swung back her hand, defiant and vengeful. But this time Logan was ready for her. His hand connected with her wrist before it reached his face, and he twisted it until she cried out with pain, then suddenly swung her up into his arms, his hands cruelly hard.

She fought him all the way to the bedroom, and when he dropped her on the bed she tried to struggle up and get away from him, but his heavy body kept her there while he captured her wrists in one hand and began undressing her—and himself—with the other. Her blouse tore when he hauled it off, and she flailed out at him with a closed fist, connecting with a hard bare chest. He gave a little grunt, but it turned to soft laughter in an instant, and she knew she hadn't hurt him at all. Her shoes had come off, and she found one of them on the bed and grabbed it, lifted it as Logan pulled at the zip on her skirt, but he raised his arm and stopped hers with it, numbing her wrist as the shoe dropped harmlessly to the floor. Her skirt followed it, and his hand caught her wrists again as he lowered himself over her, his thighs across her legs pinning them down, and his mouth finding her throat, the curve of her breast, and then finally her mouth.

His kiss was merciless, a passionate, arrogant posses-
sion, like his hold on her. It was a battle, and Raina
knew she couldn't win, but she went on struggling uselessly until she was too exhausted to fight him any
longer. When she finally lay still and her resistance
ebbed, he raised his head to look down at her, and she
felt the heaviness of his breathing against her breasts,
saw the gleam of his eyes that seemed almost wolfish in
the darkness.

'That's better,' he said, and she loathed the quiet
satisfaction in his voice.

'I can't fight you,' she said. 'I can't stop you——'

'That's right,' said Logan. 'You can't.'

She thought it was nearly over, that she only needed
to grit her teeth and hate him while he repeated the
angry, unloving act of the night they were married. But it
wasn't like that at all. His hands began to touch her
gently, caressing her body slowly and with increasing
intimacy, and his lips followed them. She felt the insistent
stirring of desire, and made a movement of protest, of escape. But his hands stopped her, and she went rigid in his
grasp, her hands clenching, her jaw going tight.

'Oh, no,' said Logan softly. 'No, darling, it won't do.'

She knew what he meant, and tried to lie as un-
responsive as a log of wood, a figure carved in stone.
His soft laughter touched her ear, and she felt his tongue
exploring the lobe, moving down the little groove below,
then lightly touching on the hollow at the base of her
throat. His fingers gently kneaded the soft flesh of her
breast, and went lower to explore the slimness of her
waist and the flat smoothness of her stomach. She trembled, and he felt it, his mouth lifting from its exploration
of her breasts, and finding hers again.

When he stopped kissing her, Raina moved her head in fretful negation denying the rising tide of passion within her body, moaning, 'No—no. Don't!'

But he was inexorable in his slow, compelling seduction, and although minutes later she still whispered, 'No—no—oh, no!' it was no longer a pathetic attempt at rejection. It was a cry of disbelief, of bewilderment, a strange cry of protest, because he had brought her to a peak of pleasure so intense she didn't know if she could bear it, a kind of refined torture of the senses that was almost terrifying in its uninhibited sensuality, and left total exhaustion in its wake, so that when the raging tide of passion receded, she floated immediately into a state of sleep so deep it was like a faint.

In the morning she woke when the first rays of the sun were pushing through the chink between the blind and the window. Raina was conscious immediately that she was not alone, and twisted involuntarily in the bed to stare at Logan's sleeping face.

Her movement must have disturbed him. He opened his eyes and they were almost immediately fully aware, as he raised himself on his elbow to look at her.

Memory flooded into her mind, her cheeks flared with colour and she turned away from him, huddling the sheet about her nakedness. She wondered if he had remembered, in the instant of waking, which woman it was who lay beside him. Had he expected to see Angela's face, perhaps, instead of his wife's?

His hand touched her bared shoulder, and she hunched away from him. Humiliation swept over her as she remembered her capitulation, her inability to hide the desire he had aroused, her final complete submission to his demands on her ... more than submission ... an eagerness and passion that in the end had matched his.

His fingers on her shoulders tightened and turned her

to face him, and he read the rejection in her face. 'What's the matter?' he asked, frowning down at her.

'Nothing,' she lied. Her head turned away from him, and she muttered, 'I want to get up.'

'In a minute,' he said, his lips brushing her shoulder, wandering across her skin. 'You're beautiful—did I tell you that last night? Beautiful and quite marvellously sexy.'

'Thank you,' she said in brittle tones. 'I'm glad I gave satisfaction. My other duties as *your wife* include making breakfast, I believe. Can I go now?'

Logan lifted his head and stared, his eyes growing slowly icy as he took in the hostility in her face. His mouth went taut and cruel, and he said, 'No. You can damn well stay here until I've finished with you!'

She struggled uselessly for a few minutes, then lay limply in his arms. He pushed away the sheet impatiently and this time there was no long, slow, unhurried preliminary. He took her quickly and without consideration. But in the final moments, when she wanted above all to show him her contempt by withholding any flicker of response, she found herself suddenly unable to resist his passion. Her mouth opened under his, and her body arched itself against him and her sharp gasps of fulfilment mingled with his at the end.

Afterwards they said nothing. Raina lay quietly, staring at the ceiling, while Logan's hands took a lingering farewell of her body, and then he slipped out of the bed and was gone. Raina held the sheet clutched uselessly across her breasts, and the ceiling shimmered crazily against her vision, because of the unshed tears in her eyes.

CHAPTER SEVEN

DANNY seemed to notice nothing amiss between Raina and Logan, perhaps because they both made special efforts to appear normal and contented in his presence. If it reminded Raina uncannily of the days when she and Logan had entered into the same kind of tacit agreement to hide their antagonism from Perry, she thrust the knowledge to the back of her mind, refusing to think through the implications. These days she was doing her best to live on the surface, and not delve too deeply into the dark recesses of memory.

Logan seemed to be determined to work them into the mould of the ideal family. He organised family outings, to a circus, to beaches, to the lake on Sundays, and he made sure that Raina came as well as Danny. They would stroll together down bush paths or along the shore of the lake or of the ocean, Danny darting ahead, and Logan with his arm about Raina's waist, and she would smile at Danny and answer Logan's casual remarks in placid tones, and avoid looking at his eyes, because they taunted her—and told her that he knew her indifference was a lie.

He no longer slept in the spare room. He shared the big bed with her, pulling her into his arms and showing her again and again that the needs of her body took little heed of the dictates of her mind. She would never turn to him willingly, and each time she fought silently until fighting was no longer possible, and the treacherous desire heated her body and she could not hide it from him. She hated her own submission, his soft, triumphant laughter when she moaned and gave her lips

131

to him, sobbed with the frustration of her determined resistance, and raised her arms to encircle his neck and pull him closer to her feverish, heedless, wanton body. She was ashamed of her obvious need of him, afraid of his power, but helpless in the face of it, when he looked at her with the knowledge of it in his eyes, and when he touched her in a certain way, his hands speaking an explicit, erotic language that her body understood too well.

Danny seemed to be growing up fast, his speech becoming more adult, his manner more confident. There were times when Raina looked at the sturdy limbs that were quickly losing their baby chubbiness, and the face that grew more like his father's every day, and caught her breath at the thought of how fleeting childhood was, how swift the transition from baby to boy, from boy to man.

She was thinking it and watching him one day when she sat with Logan on a sun-drenched beach while Danny dug hopefully for pipis at the tide's edge. There were some of the shellfish around, and Logan had helped to find a few before leaving Danny to fossick for himself.

'What is it?' Logan asked quietly, and Raina turned to see his eyes fixed on her face.

'Nothing.'

He followed her gaze back to Danny, suntanned and covered with sand, a bucket swinging from one hand and his other arm buried to the elbow in the dark wet sand as he felt for the elusive pipis. 'He's happy,' said Logan, and turned questioning eyes back to her.

'It's just—he's going to grow up so fast,' she said in a low voice.

'That's what life's all about. You don't want to lose your baby, but you have to let him go some time. It's a gradual process.'

'Untying the apron strings?' she said wryly. 'Yes. I don't think—I'm very good at it.'

'It might help if he wasn't the only one.'

Raina wouldn't look at him. Her head down on her raised knees, half hidden in the curve of her arm, she said, 'Yes, I suppose it might have.'

'I wasn't thinking in the past tense,' said Logan, his voice very dry.

She raised her head, looking out at the gentle sea, and pushed her hair back with both hands. Then she turned to look at him. 'Do you want children, Logan?'

'I'd like to think that *you* want *my* children,' he said. Raina looked away, her face shuttered, and he said with an underlying harshness, 'Well, a man's entitled to a few dreams.'

She said, 'I'm sorry.'

'Are you?' His tone was curious, and he looked at her with an almost clinical interest, as though she was a strange specimen presented for his inspection.

Raina got up and walked away from him, going down the sand to ask Danny how his shellfishing was coming along.

Angela was giving a party. Logan tossed out the information casually one evening, and told Raina they were invited.

'Is it a special occasion?' Raina asked, hiding her sudden tension.

'A housewarming,' said Logan. 'She's bought a new home—a unit.'

'You must be paying her a good salary,' Raina commented, slightly acid. 'Where did she live before?'

There was an almost imperceptible silence before he said, 'She was sharing a flat.'

An unwelcome suspicion shot into Raina's mind. 'So she'll be living alone now?' she asked.

'That's right. She's a big girl, after all.'

Big enough to set up home on her own—so that her lover could more easily visit her? Raina wondered. She didn't want to attend the party, but Logan expected her to go, and although various excuses presented themselves to her mind, she didn't think he would swallow one of them.

She did demur about leaving Danny with a strange babysitter, but Logan solved that easily. He had met Sally French when she dropped in to pick up her son on a return visit to Danny, and Sally had offered to have Danny any time for the night. Shaun was a lone child, too, and company was good for him. So at Logan's prompting Raina rang Sally who seemed genuinely pleased at the idea. Raina reminded herself she must return the favour some time.

Raina bought a new dress for the party, out of some obscure urge to look her best. Sally took Danny with her after play-centre, leaving Raina with all afternoon in which to get ready. She washed her hair and blow-dried it to silky softness, soaked in a prolonged scented bath, used all the beauty aids she possessed, and finally dressed in the sea-green romantically sophisticated dress, noting with satisfaction the way it fitted over the gentle swell of her breasts, the neckline just low enough to tantalise without a hint of vulgarity. A belt defined her narrow waist and the feminine curve of her hips, and the skirt skimmed her thighs lightly to the hem which floated about her calves.

` She slipped on high-heeled sandals and put a silver filigree bangle on her wrist, then looked critically into the mirror. She looked—all right, she decided.

The flare of admiration in Logan's eyes confirmed it when he came in, late from work and with just time for a quick shower and a hasty meal before they left. Raina hadn't eaten. She was strung up and not hungry at all. When Logan asked her if she had had something, she murmured a reply and let him think it was an affirmative. He didn't say why he was late, and she didn't ask.

Angela opened the door to them looking stunning in black satin that defined every curve and accentuated the fairness of her skin and hair. There were quite a lot of people there, some of whom Raina knew because they were connected with Logan's business. She caught one or two curious glances at her by people who had known her as Perry's wife, and not seen her since she had married Logan.

Angela seemed very gay, much less coolly poised than when Raina had first met her, and several times she caught Logan looking at their hostess with a slight frown between his brows. She had caught a look between them, when Angela first opened the door, which she could not interpret, a question unspoken in Logan's eyes, and a reassuring answer in Angela's. But Logan seemed vaguely uneasy about her, and she was sure he was counting Angela's drinks. Was he afraid of what the girl might give away, if she had a bit too much alcohol?

She was caught up in a conversation with the wife of one of the mechanics who worked for Logan, when she saw a tall, fair man with a moustache talking to Angela. Angela was smiling, a half-full glass in her hand. The man suddenly caught at her wrist, and the drink slopped with the violence of his movement, staining the black satin dress.

No one else seemed to have noticed, and the woman talking to Raina carried on without a break, but Logan suddenly made a soft exclamation under his breath, and left them, to thread his way rapidly through the chattering crowd to Angela's side.

His shoulders obscured the look on the girl's face, but Raina saw the man with her stiffen, flush and turn away, then Logan took Angela by the arm and steered her to a door and through it, closing it behind them.

Raina didn't follow them, but she felt a sudden urge to get away, and muttering some excuse to the mechanic's wife, she made for the nearest door herself. It led into the kitchen, and she stopped there, breathing quickly, until someone opened the door behind her, calling, 'Any ice in here?'

A man and a woman came in, gay, laughing and brandishing glasses. 'I don't know,' she said, gesturing vaguely to the fridge standing in a corner. 'You can look, I suppose.'

They found some, and left, and Raina opened the outer door and slipped into the cool night air.

She was in a sort of courtyard, with tubs of greenery dimly visible in the spilled light from the windows. It would be pretty in daylight, and there was a white wrought iron love-seat along one wall of the house where one could sit and enjoy the sun on a fine day.

She went to it, and sat down, resting her head back against the cold stone of the building and closing her eyes tiredly. And then she heard Logan's voice.

'Why the hell did you invite him?' he was asking roughly.

'Look, I told you, I feel nothing for him, now, Logan!

Nothing!' Angela, of course, her voice soft and distressed.

'That, Angel, is pretty hard to believe. Were you indulging in a spot of revenge?'

'Revenge? No, I don't think so. A bit of face-saving, perhaps. A bit of—flaunting of my independence, if you like. No girl likes the discovery that she comes second in a man's life to—to someone else.'

'I know. So you were showing off—and it wasn't a bad performance, though a trifle overplayed, I thought. One thing's rather obvious. Your ex-boy-friend isn't as indifferent to you as you claim you are to him. You could probably have him back any time you wanted.'

'I *don't*!' Angela cried. 'I don't care if I never see him again!'

'True?'

'True!'

'Okay. I must say I'm delighted to hear it. There, that's about the best I can do with your dress, I think. Will it stain?'

'Probably. It's new, too, but never mind. I don't know that I would have wanted to wear it again.'

There was a short pause, then Angela said, 'How do you like the way I've fixed the place?'

'Very nice. But you don't need my opinion. You have a talent for decorating.'

'I'd like to know that you approve, though. After all, a good deal of your money has gone into it.'

'It wasn't so much, and it's worth it, if you're happy.'

They were moving away, and Raina couldn't hear Angela's reply to that. The light spilling from the window nearby—the bathroom, she presumed—or was it Angela's bedroom?—had disappeared as someone flicked off the switch, and she sat staring numbly into the darkness, afraid to move, afraid to think.

It seemed she sat there a long time, but when she finally got up and stumbled to the kitchen door, blinking stupidly at the light when she opened it, only ten minutes or so had elapsed. A man came in as she closed the door behind her, and he grinned and said something that she didn't hear.

He rinsed a couple of glasses at the sink, then, holding them in one hand, opened the door with the other and waited for her to go through. Raina smiled at him automatically and went back into the noise of the party. Angela was passing round plates of savouries, and the fair man with the moustache seemed to have disappeared. She saw Logan looking over the shoulder of someone who was standing talking to him, and when he saw her he excused himself with a word and made his way over to her.

'Are you all right?' he asked her in a low voice.

'Yes,' she said. 'Shouldn't I be?'

'What have you been doing?'

'I went out to the kitchen for a glass of water,' she said. 'And some fresh air. It's stuffy in here.'

'We can go home, soon ... You're not enjoying the party, are you?'

'Not particularly. I can go home alone, if you want to stay.' She spoke calmly, not looking at him.

'We'll go together,' he said. 'After supper's over.'

When they said goodnight to Angela, she looked more relaxed than she had when they arrived. She caught Logan's arm briefly and murmured something to him as Raina was turning towards the door. Raina saw Logan's hand quickly cover the girl's, and he smiled down at her before joining Raina and opening the door for her.

Raina stared out at the dark streets, splashed with light from the street lamps, as Logan drove them home. They crossed one of the graceful bridges over the broad gleam of the river, and entered the quiet tree-lined street where Logan's house was.

Logan's house. Not really hers, but Logan's. As, apparently, Angela's house was Logan's, too, bought with his money, for his—mistress.

She stood in front of the dressing table and slipped off the bracelet on her arm, as Logan removed his jacket and tie and unbuttoned his shirt. He sat down on the bed to take off his shoes, and looked up at her, his eyes meeting hers in the mirror.

Raina looked away immediately, but he came up behind her, placed his hands on her hips and pulled her back against him, his lips nuzzling the curve of her neck.

Raina stiffened, her back going rigid, her hands clenched. Logan's head came up and again their reflected eyes met, his sparkling with anger, and hers with hatred.

She heard him draw in a harsh breath, and then he turned her to face him, and bent her head back with a savage kiss. His fingers bit into her shoulders, and her neck ached with the pressure he exerted.

Her hands pushed at him, beat against his shoulders, but the kiss went on and on, until she was dizzy and breathless, the taste of his mouth, the heat of his body the only things of which she was conscious in the whole world. His arms gathered her closer to him until it seemed she was being enveloped by him, drowned in his merciless passion, and the only protest she could make was a small, sobbing whimper in her throat.

When Logan heard it, he broke the kiss, his breathing uneven and loud as he still held her, his eyes blazing on to her face so that she flinched and turned her head aside. 'Let me go,' she whispered in a shaken voice. 'I hate you!'

'Hate?' he taunted. 'Is it hate when you stop fighting me and put your arms round my neck to pull me closer to you? When you tip back your head against the pillow and open your mouth for my kisses? When you press your fingers into my hair and hold me to your breast? When you arch your body under mine and beg me to——'

'*Stop it!*' she cried tensely. 'Stop it!'

'Actions speak louder than words,' he said, and lifted her and took her over to the bed.

She didn't fight, this time. But she held the thought of the conversation she had overhead, in her mind, and played it over and over like a recording. She lay passive and unresisting in his arms. With a sense of bitter triumph, she remained remote and unfeeling while Logan's passion rose and spent itself against her deliberate coldness. When he rolled away from her, his breathing loud and quick, hers was still even and quiet, her body cool and no more sentient than a doll's.

When he spoke his voice was thick and harsh. 'All right, Raina, you win,' he said. 'That's the last time you make me feel like a rapist. From now on, you can sleep alone.'

She felt the bed lighten as he got up, and heard the rustle of his clothes. He opened the door and stopped there. 'It's ironic,' he said. 'All this determined fidelity of yours, to a man who wasn't even faithful to you when he was alive!'

The door slammed behind him, and Raina closed her eyes tightly, the echo of his words thundering in her mind. It wasn't true—it couldn't be true. Perry couldn't have been unfaithful to her. He *couldn't* have . . .

The morning was grey and windblown, with cold spurts of rain flinging now and then against the windows. It matched Raina's mood, and she had to force herself to leave her bed and get dressed.

Logan was standing in the kitchen when she got there, leaning on the sink counter in front of the window, as though he had been waiting for her. His eyes looked grey like the high, rainwashed clouds beyond the glass, and there was a bleakness in his face she had seen before, a long time ago, so that she looked away from him, not wanting to see it, not wanting to know what it meant.

'Have you had breakfast?' she asked him, turning to pull out the toaster and open the bread bin. She didn't want toast, but she had to do something to avoid meeting his eyes, to keep her hands occupied.

'I've had all I want,' he said. 'Raina, I'm sorry about last night. I probably drank too much, and—I had no right to say that about Perry.'

He hadn't drunk very much last night, he had been too busy watching what Angela was drinking. And Raina had never known drink to affect him in any visible way. She put down the loaf of bread carefully on the laminated surface of the counter and turned to face him. 'Are you telling me it was a lie?' she asked, her eyes on his face.

He straightened up, and a muscle in his jaw tightened, moving under his tanned skin. The short silence was intense, then he said, 'Yes, it was a lie. I was angry, and I wanted to hurt you. I won't ask you to forgive me.'

She looked into his eyes and knew that he was trying to keep them free of expression, but she saw what he wanted to hide. He had one hand on the counter just behind him, and his fist was clenched on the surface, the knuckles showing white.

He said, 'I have to go.'

Only then he took his eyes from hers and went over

to the door. He was almost there when Raina said, her eyes on the window with the rain blurring the glass, drops chasing each other endlessly down the pane, 'Logan.'

'Yes?' he said, turning his head slowly, almost as though he was reluctant to be delayed by her.

'Thank you,' she whispered.

She didn't see the look on his face, only sensed his odd stillness before he inclined his dark head briefly, almost jerkily, and then went out.

Raina had arranged to pick up Danny after lunch, and the morning dragged. The house seemed dark and oppressive, and about eleven she could stand it no longer. She put on boots and a raincoat and went for a walk, aimlessly, but she ended on a path that wound along the riverbank, shorn grass between the path and the sluggish, dark green water, and oaks shushing their leaves in the wind overhead.

She sat on a park bench overlooking the river, and while droplets of water spattered down on her head with every gust of wind from the tree behind her, and a blue-plumaged pukeko stalked among the reeds at the river's edge, she watched the dark rippling eddies and tried to think of nothing at all . . .

It wasn't possible, of course, and small snatches of memory kept floating into her mind, until at last she abandoned the attempt to keep them at bay, and gave way to the flood.

Perry when he first met her, when she had been having a drink with the man who had taught her to fly, celebrating the fact that she had passed her solo test with flying colours. Perry taking her up, later, in his plane, showing her how to do aerobatics, admiration in his eyes when she followed his instructions without turning a hair, when she laughed at him as he tried to frighten her by throwing the plane into a spin or a barrel roll without warning. Perry leaning on the counter of the airlines office where she worked as a receptionist, grinning at her and teasing her about doing such a mundane job.

'I'm not qualified for anything much,' she had told him. 'This is the nearest I can get to actually flying.'

'I'll take you flying,' he said, his eyes full of impudent meaning. And he had, they had flown together, laughed and loved, and it had all been glorious and beautiful and they had had their happy-ever-after ending. Except that it hadn't lasted for ever ...

When Danny came, she had stopped flying. Danny took a lot of time, and she wouldn't go up with Perry any more, in case the baby lost both parents at once. Perry laughed and teased her for her caution, but Raina wouldn't budge.

There had been business trips, delivery flights, when he tried to coax her to come along. But she didn't enjoy that sort of thing much, and there was always Danny, troublesome to take along, and she didn't like to leave him. Perry would part from her with a kiss and come back laughing and with his arms full of presents for her and Danny.

'Logan will keep an eye on you,' he would say as he left, and when he came back, 'Logan looked after you, didn't he?'

And Raina would say, 'Yes.' Logan would have phoned at least once, perhaps called in for ten minutes on his way to or from the airfield. 'Let me know if you need anything,' he would say. 'Perry asked me to watch out for you ...'

Raina managed all right on her own. She said so to Perry, often, and he would kiss her cheek and say coaxingly, 'For my sake—I feel better if I know Logan's in charge.'

'*I'm* in charge!' she said crossly, once. 'Logan's just a—spare wheel, in case I break a leg or something!'

Perry shouted with laughter. 'Okay,' he grinned. 'I must tell Logan that—! I wonder how he'll like being called a spare wheel!'

Once she told Logan to forget the whole deal. 'I can't,' he said. 'Perry trusts me.'

Raina looked up swiftly, then, and something unspoken passed between them, bringing a faint flush to Raina's cheeks and making Logan suddenly sharp-eyed and tight-lipped.

'It isn't necessary,' she said. 'I'm quite all right on my own.'

'I know that,' he said. 'So does Perry. But he likes to think of you as being in need of his protection.'

'Or yours?'

'I'm protecting Perry,' said Logan. 'That's how he wants it. He likes to think of me being his proxy, in his absence—as far as it goes.'

'As far as it goes?' she echoed. 'What do you mean?'

'I mean, he wouldn't want me to claim the privileges of a husband.'

'There's no question of your being allowed to!' Raina flashed.

'There's no question of my trying to,' he answered. 'And Perry knows it. He knows us both very well, Raina.'

She hadn't wanted to understand what he meant, had thrust the conversation into the deepest recesses of her mind.

She had never broken a leg, but there had been a time, not during one of Perry's absences, when she had twisted her ankle . . .

She had gone out to the airfield, taking Danny with her, to pick up Perry. They had only one car, and Logan was supposed to have left early that day, meaning that he would be unable to drop Perry off. Raina had taken Danny to the doctor for one of his vaccinations and had needed the car.

Logan was still there when she arrived; he had been held up, after all. They all left together, Logan holding the door, swinging the keys in his hand as Perry went out with Danny in his arms, and Raina suddenly hesitated and said, 'I've left Danny's juice bottle on Perry's desk.'

She turned back to get it, and Perry called, 'I'll get Danny into the car seat.' It was a good safety guard, but the straps took time to do up, with a wriggling baby to contend with.

Raina scooped up the empty bottle, and passed Logan hastily as he stood waiting for her, his hand on the door. Too hastily—her high heel caught in one of the slats of the wooden steps, and she stumbled, wrenching her ankle painfully and losing her shoe. Her heart lurched as she began falling, then a strong, hard arm came about her, and she clutched thankfully at the lapel of Logan's jacket, her face against his shirt, his thighs touching hers.

The bottle clattered down the steps, but she heard only the deep thuds of Logan's heart, the quick intake of his breath as her softness, clamped against him, melted into the hard planes of his body. He shifted his feet slightly, and it seemed to bring them even closer. For a long, silent moment they stayed like that, his chin against her hair, her hands flattened on his chest. Then he asked, 'Are you all right?'

It was an effort to answer. Her heart raced and her lips were suddenly trembling. 'Yes,' she said at last.

She made no attempt to move, and for a little longer he held her closely before his hands gradually relaxed their hold, and his arms fell slowly away. Raina raised her eyes to his, wide with shock, bewildered and a little frightened.

His answering look was sombre, deeply penetrating, and she shivered.

'It's all right,' said Logan. 'You're safe. Nothing happened.'

He stooped and picked up her shoe, said, 'Here you are, Cinderella,' in his normal, half-mocking tones, and, while she put it on, closed the door and went down the steps to retrieve the dropped bottle.

She had to lean on the railing at the side of the steps because her ankle hurt when she put her weight on it. He waited for her on the path below, and turned to walk beside her to the car-park behind the building. She limped a little, although she tried not to. But Logan didn't offer to help her, just walked along beside her in silence until they reached the car. Danny was strapped in, gurgling happily, and Perry had slid in behind the wheel. Logan opened the passenger door for Raina, handed her the bottle, slanted them both his familiar, lazy smile and went off with a casual wave of his hand to his own car.

Starting the car, Perry queried, 'Something wrong, Raina? You look rather pale.'

'I ricked my ankle,' she said. 'It hurts a bit.'

He was concerned and insisted on looking at it, found a slight swelling and suggested taking her to a doctor.

Raina said, 'No, I can walk on it. Take me home, Perry.'

He took her home and made her rest with a cold compress pressed about the swelling. He fed Danny himself and put him to bed, and later carried her to bed, too, and sank down on the mattress beside her, kissing her helplessly. They made love, and she clung to him with an almost desperate passion, seeking the total physical culmination that would blot out uneasiness, obliterate fear, erase an unfounded sense of guilt.

The rain was falling steadily now, dancing droplets spreading rippling skirts in the water, and making a muted drumming on the leaves of the tree. Raina realised that her hair was soaked, and a cold trickle ran down the back of her neck into her collar.

She shivered and got up, raising splashes of water with her shoes as she hurried back along the path.

She changed her clothes and heated up a tin of soup for her belated lunch, then it was time to collect Danny. Thank heaven for Danny, who didn't notice undercurrents of tension, who kept a frail barrier of concern for him between herself and Logan, and acted as a damper on explosive situations.

Danny was blessedly normal, chattering about Shaun's toys, Shaun's bedroom, Shaun's house. He sat in the kitchen and helped her to make biscuits, which she did more to keep him occupied than because they needed any. She felt almost ready to greet Logan with a semblance of serenity by the time she was sitting Danny up at the table for his evening meal. But the phone rang and Angela's cool voice informed her that Logan had asked her to tell Raina he would be late.

'Did he say why?' she asked automatically.

There was tiny, telling silence, then Angela said, 'No, he didn't say, Mrs Thorne. Just that he doesn't know what time he'll be home.'

Raina thanked her and hung up, with an unshakeable conviction that Angela knew exactly why Logan was going to be late.

She went to bed quite early, read until midnight and then switched out the bedside lamp.

When she got up she cast a glance into the spare room, to find the bed untouched. But when she went into the kitchen Logan was sitting there, hunched over a cup of coffee. He looked up, and she saw the grey weariness in his face, the dark shadow of unshaven beard on his jaw.

He might have been with Angela, of course. But his face shocked her. His eyes looked strangely glittery, and his mouth was grim.

'What is it?' she asked.

'Nothing,' he said. 'Nothing to do with you.'

The phone rang, and he jumped up as though he had expected it, knocking over his chair in his eagerness to answer it.

Raina heard him say, 'Yes?' and then, his voice dropping, 'I see. Yes—let's hope. Thanks.'

When he came back, she said, 'You've been up all night, haven't you?'

'Yes,' he said wearily. 'I had to come home to catch some sleep.'

She said, 'Tell me.'

He looked at her and said abruptly, 'Les is overdue. He was flying over the Kaimais, should have been back at the airfield by late afternoon.'

'Les,' she said. She remembered a big curly-headed man with prominent teeth, who had been flying for the company for a couple of years now. 'Angela didn't tell me,' she said.

'I didn't want you to know. That's why I didn't ring you myself. A well-trained secretary doesn't divulge any more than she's told to.'

'You stayed at the office?'

'Yes. They organised search parties last night, went

out this morning at first light. I waited at the office until someone else came in to take calls. That was Angela—she's just heard, they've spotted what might be some wreckage.'

Raina sat down. 'How long—before they reach it?' she asked.

'Maybe an hour or two. It depends on the terrain. They're sending a rescue party. The weather there is bad—they can't get aircraft up.'

'The wreckage——? Was there any sign of—Les?'

'No signs of life,' Logan said harshly. His hands lay on the table, clenched on either side of his cup, and Raina suddenly reached over to put her own hands on them.

He looked up, surprise in his eyes, and opened his palms, took her fingers in them.

'You couldn't have done anything last night,' she said. 'Why didn't you come home?'

'At first, in case he came in after all. Then—I didn't want the call to come here.'

If Les was dead, he meant. He hadn't wanted her to be reminded of what had happened to Perry. Raina looked down at their hands lying together on the table, and remembered how he had closed his fingers over hers in the coroner's courtroom. 'You've been there alone, all night?' she said softly.

'Angela hung about until midnight. Then I sent her home.'

She stayed there, staring at his long tanned fingers encircling hers. Then she withdrew her hands quite slowly from his grasp and stood up. 'You need more than coffee,' she said. 'I'll cook you some bacon and eggs.'

Logan didn't go to bed, but showered and shaved after he had eaten, then played with Danny, who was thrilled to have him unexpectedly home.

'You should sleep,' Raina told him.

But he said, 'I'll wait a bit longer. I don't think I could sleep, anyway.'

When the call came, Raina switched off the vacuum cleaner that she was using, and stood staring at the phone. Logan passed her, snatched up the receiver, and only seconds later was putting it down, leaning a hand against the wall for a moment, then turning to look at Raina.

She looked at the blaze of light in his eyes, and began to shake.

'He's all right!' Logan said. 'A broken leg, concussion, maybe some cracked ribs, that's all. He'll be fine.'

'Yes,' she said, and wound her arms about her body, trying to stop the stupid shivering. 'Yes.'

He hauled her into his arms, holding her hard and close, and she saw Danny standing staring at her, his eyes wide with surprise. She clamped her teeth tightly, took a deep, shuddering breath and pulled away, going to her son, sinking to her knees beside him. 'It's all right, darling. Mummy's just a bit cold, that's all.'

'Was Uncle Logan making you warm?'

'Yes.'

Danny dropped the toy car he was holding and put his thin arms about her, hugging her tightly.

'Oh, Danny!' she said, and stood up, taking him with her, returning the hug. 'You're sweet!'

'Uncle Logan too!' Danny said.

Raina caught Logan's eye over the child's shoulder, and found him giving her a sardonic look. 'Yes,' she said, laughter in her voice, 'Uncle Logan, too.'

Again she caught surprise in Logan's eyes, and his mouth softened at the corners, almost smiling. 'I'm going to be even sweeter,' he said, 'and make you a hot drink. Want one, Danny?'

She sat in the kitchen with Danny beside her, and Logan made cocoa, milky and sweet. When Danny had drunk his and gone off to retrieve the discarded car and carry on with the block roads he was building in the lounge, Raina said, 'I don't know what came over me.'

'Reaction,' said Logan. 'Not just to Les's accident—to a lot of other things, some of them going way back . . . You never went to pieces like that when Perry died, did you?'

Raina shook her head. That was the ridiculous part. She hardly knew Les, couldn't even recall his last name. She didn't understand her own emotional response to the news. Logan was probably right. She had always slightly despised women who suffered from 'nerves'. But quite possibly she was becoming one of them, herself.

It was a ghastly thought, and almost defensively, she said, 'I'm not a neurotic type.'

Logan's sudden laughter was almost reassuring.

'Don't I know it!' he said. 'I wasn't suggesting it for a minute. You're not neurotic, Raina—just stubborn and brave and sometimes—sometimes decidedly infuriating.' He paused, then leaned over the table a little, his hand imprisoning hers. 'For God's sake, stop fighting me, Raina,' he said. 'I know I've handled—things—badly. But I want—I want to work it out, and I think you do, too, even if it's only for Daniel's sake. I've told you, you can sleep alone if that's what you want. I swear I'll make no more demands on you in that sphere . . . not until you want it.'

Was he getting all he needed *in that sphere*, elsewhere? she wondered bitterly. *Why* had he married her, and not Angela? He had said, not for Perry's sake, or Danny's.

Was it because Angela gave him what he wanted without a wedding ring, and he had realised that Raina wouldn't? For a moment she felt a swift jab of pity for Angela. She must be very much in love with either Logan or his money. *No woman likes to know she comes second to someone else*, she had said. That made Raina first, she supposed. It didn't make her feel any better.

'Why did you marry me?' she asked baldly.

'Why?' Logan frowned, his eyes looking unfocused, and she realised that he was deathly tired. 'For God's sake, woman!' he said, his voice thick with exhaustion. 'I loved you—and I'd been tortured long enough. I didn't know—it could get worse.'

CHAPTER EIGHT

RAINA sat dumb, feeling nothing but a kind of dull shock.

Logan was getting to his feet, almost stumbling, pushing at the table to lever himself up. 'I'm going to bed,' he muttered.

He almost tripped over Danny in the doorway, his hand fleetingly closing on the boy's shoulder.

'Uncle Logan——' Danny began, and Raina said gently, 'Come here, Danny. Uncle Logan's very tired.'

A rubber tire had worked its way off the metal wheel of the car, and she forced herself to concentrate on getting it back, and listen to Danny's description of his 'roads'.

She tried to keep him quiet for the rest of the day, while Logan slept. It wasn't easy, and when the rain finally cleared in the late afternoon and a watery sun dried the ground in patches, she took Danny out for a walk.

When they returned there was a note on the table from Logan. He had gone back to the office, and might not be home until late.

Raina supposed he had things to catch up on, and there were probably arrangements to be made, and decisions to do with the wrecked plane. She read the note again, and its brief impersonality bothered her. There was no greeting, no ending. Just 'Raina——' at the beginning, and his name scrawled at the end.

I loved you, he had said, before he stumbled away to sleep off his exhaustion. Had he meant that in the past tense? And he had said something about 'torture'.

Pain twisted inside her, remembering the look on his face, the look of a man who had taken enough, who was at the end of his tether. *I'd been tortured long enough*, he had said. *I didn't know it could get worse.*

He was tired, she told herself, he scarcely knew what he was saying. But she knew that he had been speaking some stark truth, and it was a truth that she had been trying to avoid for a long time.

It had been there when she married Perry, and Logan had kissed her. It had been there when she told herself that she disliked him, that she tolerated him in their home because he was Perry's friend, and when she and Logan had both hidden their antagonism from Perry, camouflaged their intense awareness of each other, Logan with a lazy mockery and Raina with a cool indifference. Antagonism—yes, there had been that, because at first neither of them had wanted to acknowledge the reason for the electricity that filled the air between them. Raina told herself that her skin prickled when he came near her because she couldn't stand his nearness, that her heightened consciousness of her every movement when he was about was because she knew how critically he watched her.

And she knew he did watch her, even though she seldom raised her eyes to his. She knew that he watched her so much he must know her body almost as intimately as Perry did—as intimately as any man could who had never touched her. And she thrust away the fierce, prideful, malicious pleasure that rose in her at the thought. Thrust down her knowledge of why he watched her, and why she liked it that he did. It didn't matter that frequently his eyes were coldly critical, or strangely resentful, sometimes even contemptuous or amused. Because behind that there was always something else—reluctant, nearly hidden, but there all the same. She called it admiration because she wouldn't give it the name of—desire.

Logan didn't like her—he didn't trust her to love Perry as he thought Perry deserved—but he couldn't keep that look from his eyes. They both pretended that it wasn't there, and only once, when he had nettled her more than usual with his sarcasm, the sarcasm he used as a weapon against her, she had deliberately held his eyes with hers in a long, knowing look that made his eyes narrow suddenly, and a tiny muscle jump briefly in his lean cheek.

She had surprised him, and she was satisfied. Satisfied that she had the upper hand, and that he knew it—until that day when he had caught her close when she tripped on the steps, and he had soothed her sudden fright with totally unexpected gentleness in his voice. He hadn't been talking about her fall, about her physical safety, when he said, *'You're safe. Nothing happened.'* She had known quite clearly what he meant, and what the danger had been.

And she knew that after that day there had been a change. She had banished the incident to the back of her mind, refusing to examine its significance. And she had become even more cool, even a little waspish to Logan, so that Perry had laughingly protested, slightly shocked. But Logan smiled tolerantly and refused to rise to her baiting. He was gentler than he had been, less sharp-edged, his mockery not so pointed, his glance less rapier-like, and frequently veiled by half-closed lids.

'You've mellowed him, Raina!' said Perry after a while, and laughed.

'Everyone mellows with age,' she said. 'Even Logan.'

'I feel like Methuselah,' said Logan. 'I'm about the same age as Perry is, Raina.'

Of course he was, virtually, but he always seemed

years older. Perry was a kind of Peter Pan, eternally boyish. It was one of the dearest things about him. Perry didn't change.

I loved you, Logan had said. Had he stopped loving her, since their marriage? Had she driven him away, into Angela's arms, with her coldness, her rejection?

He had said he wanted their marriage to work out . . . Did that mean he was willing to break with Angela? Or did his promise to make no demands mean that he was willing to settle for a loveless marriage, a convenient fiction for Danny's benefit? Perhaps he had decided that it was the best he could hope for—or that it was all he wanted, after all.

At midnight she gave up waiting for him to come home, and went to bed. Logan was in the bathroom when she got up, and the bed in the spare room was tumbled, his pyjamas lying on top of the blankets. Raina made breakfast, and when he came in he looked handsome and vital, perhaps a trifle less tanned than usual, as though he retained a slight pallor of exhaustion, and his expression was remote, his eyes hard as blue glass.

Raina's heart sank. She said, 'Hello, Logan,' her voice soft and husky, her eyes pleading.

But he wasn't looking at her eyes. His glance on the table, he asked, 'Can I do anything?'

'No,' she said. 'Everything's ready.'

'You're very efficient, aren't you?' he commented, his voice light and impersonal. 'Perry trained you well.'

That hurt, and she knew it had been meant to. She dug trembling hands into the pockets of her robe, and said, 'If you've finished with the bathroom, I'll get dressed.'

She locked the bathroom door and washed the hot, stinging tears from her eyes with cold water. By the time she had showered and changed into a shirt and jeans, Logan had left the house.

In the days that followed, he frustrated every attempt she made to close the distance between them. He was busy, or he was helping Danny with some project, or he had to go out. And when they were, on rare occasions, alone, he reverted to the sharp, satirical manner which she had always hated. All her determination to have things out with him and clarify the situation in which they found themselves, faltered and broke against the barrier of his cool mockery. It confused and angered her, and instead of remaining calm and forcing him into a rational discussion of their marriage and its future, she would retaliate with verbal barbs of her own. And Logan would laugh, as though that was what he had wanted all along, as though he found her hurt frustration amusing.

Sometimes Raina suspected that his jibes were a defence to hide his feelings from her, but she could find no hint of tenderness in his eyes, and even the savage, reluctant desire was absent. And then there was the thought of Angela to haunt her, to check an occasional impulse to demand frankness from Logan. Because if she forced him to make a choice, he might choose Angela.

Logan had bought Danny a toy helicopter, an amazing bit of miniature engineering that was battery-powered and actually lifted off the ground, blades whirring, and flew for short distances at a height of a few feet. Danny loved it, and it led to his badgering Logan to take him up one day, let him try out the real thing. He would, Logan said, but Raina would have to come too.

He drove them out to the airfield one fine Saturday morning, and they walked to the helicopter that stood waiting on the grass, a bright red, squat machine tapering to a slender tail at the rear.

'It's small!' Danny pronounced, inspecting it critically, touching the perspex bubble-front.

'It's big enough,' said Logan, opening up the door to lift Danny inside. The odour of weedkiller pervaded the little aircraft, and Raina grimaced a little as she followed Danny on to the bench seat. The perspex door was closed beside her, and Logan came round to hoist himself into the pilot's seat.

'What's that?' Danny asked, pointing to the bank of controls before them. Logan pointed out the fuel and oil pressure gauges and airspeed indicator, but he had only covered half the dials when Danny evidently lost interest in the mechanics of the journey, and demanded to know when they were going to fly.

Logan grinned and said, 'Now, sport.'

He turned the key, engaging the clutch, and Danny looked up as the rotor blades began slowly swinging round, then gradually gained speed.

The cockpit vibrated, and Danny squealed as the craft seemed to momentarily tip forward before it lifted off the ground, which began to fall away beneath them with breathtaking speed. Logan lifted his foot from the pedal before him, and they skimmed over the airfield buildings, the draught created by the blades bending a treetop before them as they left the field and cruised over fenced paddocks. Danny had clutched his stomach as they rose, and his eyes dilated when he gazed down and saw the incredible space between his dangling feet and the green trees and grass as the craft hovered over them, but with Raina's hand on his shoulder he soon relaxed, craning eagerly forward to watch the countryside slide away below.

After ten minutes, Logan turned and headed back to

the airfield, descended, and settled gently back on the ground. Raina let out a sharp sigh, and Logan looked at her and said in a low voice, '*You* weren't nervous, were you?'

'Not exactly,' she said. 'But it's different from a plane, isn't it?'

'It's the nearest thing to growing wings,' said Logan.

'Yes.' Apart from the drag and pull of the ascent and descent, once the machine was aloft it had a weightless feeling, as though it rode the air as lightly as a paper boat might ride on the surface of water.

'You never went in a 'copter with Perry?' Logan asked.

'No,' she said. 'You only went into helicopters after Danny was born, and I wouldn't——'

'I remember,' Logan said quietly.

The blades were slowing, the shadow on the ground not any longer an indistinct blur, but a moving succession of long oar-shapes, passing over the grass.

Logan pushed the door and got out, and Raina sat with her arm still about her son, feeling strangely shocked, as he walked around to open the other door and let them out.

She stumbled down into Logan's arms, and Danny jumped out himself, with a triumphant little grunt of satisfaction, and ran off over the grass, not waiting for them.

Logan steadied Raina slowly, his eyes on hers, watchful and enigmatic. She stared back at him, her own eyes wide with questioning and a kind of surprise. And he said, 'Thank you.'

He was thanking her for having faith in him, for trusting him not to put her and Danny at risk. She shook her head slightly, puzzled at herself, unwilling to read all the implications, and eased herself away. Logan's hands dropped and they turned together to walk back to the buildings. Outside the office Danny wheeled, his arms outstretched, watching his shadow on the grass and making roaring noises.

'He's a helicopter,' said Logan as he opened the door for Raina. 'We'll have a new craze on our hands.'

She smiled absently and walked past him into the empty office. The typewriter stood covered with grey plastic on Angela's desk, the typing chair neatly parked in front of it. They went through into the inner room. Logan had said he had about an hour's paperwork to catch up on before he took them home.

'Want a drink?' he asked.

'I'll make some tea. Do you want some?'

'Thanks. Can you find everything?'

'I'm sure I will,' she said. No doubt Angela had all the necessary ingredients in proper order.

She did, and there was even half a bottle of milk in the small refrigerator. Raina filled two of the pretty floral china cups and took them into Logan's office. He put down the pen in his hand and gestured to her to sit down opposite the desk.

He sipped his tea, watching her, and she had the curious impression that he was taking pleasure in having her sitting here with him. Her cup made a faint clatter as she replaced it in the saucer, and she stayed with her head bent, looking at it.

'How would you like to fly a helicopter?' Logan asked her.

Raina looked up. 'I don't know. It would be—a change.'

'A challenge?'

'That, too, I suppose.'

From outside the sound of Danny's humming helicopter imitation came faintly. 'Danny loved it,' she said. 'Though he was a bit scared at first.'

'A new experience is often rather frightening.'

'He'd flown before. Was he scared when you took him up in the plane?'

'As you said, it's not quite the same. You've flown before, too. You said it was different. Did you find it better than conventional flight?'

'Just different. Must I make a comparison?'

'I wish you wouldn't. Life offers a lot of new experiences. It's a mistake to keep comparing them with the ones that have gone before. You've never been afraid of accepting a challenge before.'

He wasn't talking about flying. Raina put her cup and saucer on the desk, and said, 'I'm not afraid now. I'm just not sure of what the challenge is.'

Logan's eyebrows rose a little, and his mouth expressed a wry disbelief.

He shrugged with a hint of impatience, drained his cup and replaced it on the saucer.

'I won't keep you long,' he said, and picked up the pen again.

It was an inconclusive end to the conversation, and as she washed the cups up in the small, spotless, stainless steel sink provided in the compact little kitchen off Angela's office, Raina sighed with frustration.

Danny came clattering in, and she found some ice cubes to drop in a glass of water for him. He drained the glass and popped one of the ice cubes into his cheek, then went outside again to swing on the railing guarding the steps.

The hour dragged. Raina walked about the permissible perimeters of the airfield with Danny and tried to answer his questions, then sat in the outer office while he drew pictures of airplanes on some old letterhead paper that Logan gave him. The office was bright and airy and tasteful, and it reminded her of Angela.

When at last Logan said he was finished, she stood up so quickly that he was amused. 'Bored?' he asked.

'Incredibly,' she answered crisply. 'I should have brought a book.'

'Angela keeps some magazines for visitors,' he said. 'You should have asked.'

'I wasn't to know, was I? Although Angela's such a paragon, I suppose I should have guessed.'

She swept out of the building, ignoring his narrowed gaze, taking Danny with her.

Danny sat in the back chattering, and Raina kept her eyes strictly on the view as Logan drove them home. She was so far away that it was a few moments before she reacted to Danny's sudden startled wail, and turned in her seat to see what on earth was the matter.

Drops of scarlet blood spattered his yellow tee-shirt, and for a moment her heart lurched in sickening fear, before she realised it was only his nose bleeding.

She leaned over, trying to reassure him, and Logan brought the car to a halt at the verge of the road, saying, 'What's the trouble?'

Raina gave Danny her handkerchief and said, 'Here, darling, hold that.' Then she threw open her door and scrambled into the back seat with Danny, laying his head back against her breast and explaining that it was only a nosebleed and nothing to worry about.

Danny gulped, and she said, 'It will stop soon,' but her handkerchief was soaked, and she said to Logan, 'There's a packet of tissues in the glove-box, I think. Can you get them?'

He rummaged, swore under his breath and eventually

produced them, and in a few minutes the bleeding stopped, and a relieved little boy was taken into the front
seat to sit by Raina for the remainder of the journey.
Logan's look registered sardonic disapproval, but
he said nothing in the face of Raina's challenging
stare.

She put Danny to bed early, and found Logan in the
lounge afterwards pouring himself a drink.

'Want one?' he asked her, and she said, 'Yes, that
would be nice.'

His look held faint sarcasm, but he poured a sherry
for her in silence, and handed it to her as she sat down
in one of the wide leather chairs. She ran her fingers
along the arm of the chair and absently looked about
the room as she shifted uncomfortably.

Logan asked, 'What's the matter?'

'Nothing. Your chairs are bit—overwhelming for me,
that's all.'

'You can redecorate the house, if you like.'

Rawly, she said, 'I'll leave that to Angela.'

He had been standing near the hearth, swirling his
drink absently in his glass. Suddenly it stilled. 'What do
you have against Angela?'

'Not a thing. She has good taste. She redecorated the
office, didn't she?'

'Yes. I remember you saying it was "very nice". You
haven't been to the office since then, have you—until
today?'

'No.'

'Then—what does this mean?'

Her eyes dilated as he thrust a piece of paper in front
of her, the black, official print at the top blurring before
them.

'Where did you get that?' she demanded sharply, her
mouth dry.

'It fell out of the glove-box when I was looking for those tissues. At the time I didn't realise whose it was, and I shoved it in my pocket to sort out later.'

Raina put out her hand to take it from him. 'I'd forgotten about it,' she said. She smoothed the crumpled sheet out on her knee. 'Are you going to play the heavy husband and read me the Riot Act for getting a speeding ticket?'

'Don't play games with me, Raina!' His voice was harsh with exasperation. 'What interests me is what you were doing on *that* road, on *that* day.'

'Why?' she asked desperately. 'It's a public road, and—is there anything special about that day?'

'Nothing that I recall—except that you *didn't* come to see *me*. And that road may be public, but I know the only reason you could have been on it was because you were on your way to or from the airfield.'

'What are you accusing me of, Logan? An assignation with one of your mechanics?'

She took a gulp of her sherry, and as she lowered the glass, his hand suddenly came out and took it from her. He deposited it on the mantelpiece and put his with it, glaring down into her indignant eyes. 'I'm not accusing you of anything. I just want to know why you went to the trouble of driving all that way off for nothing.'

'How do you know it was for nothing?' she said. 'I could have any number of reasons for going that way.'

'Name one.'

She stared at him, her mind a total blank.

Logan laughed. 'You had one of two reasons for going out there,' he said. 'Me—or Perry.'

'It wasn't Perry!' she cried quickly.

'I hoped—I thought it wasn't,' he said. 'I figured

you'd laid those ghosts the first time. Why were you coming to see me?'

'It wasn't important,' she shrugged. 'I don't remember. You—you were busy, I didn't want to disturb you.'

'You didn't even come into the office!' he said. 'Angela would have told me.'

Raina suddenly got to her feet, her eyes blazing green fire. 'Angela seemed pretty busy, too!' she snapped, and turned away from him, making for the door.

She never reached it. Logan's hand caught her arm and gripped it hard, turning her to face him.

'What do you mean?' he asked, but she could see the light dawning behind his eyes, the wheels of memory clicking into place. 'Busy—doing what?'

Well, if he wanted it spelled out, she would oblige. *'Kissing you!'* she said viciously. 'And being kissed! Now let me *go!*'

He didn't. He said, 'Angela has never kissed me in her life. And for the record, I haven't kissed her.'

Her eyes wide, she said, 'I *saw* you. Don't lie——'

Logan grabbed her other arm, and swung her around to shove her back into the chair. He leaned over her, full of menace, but his voice was remarkably pleasant.

'Tell me what you saw—' he said, '—*exactly!*'

'You—and Angela,' she said sullenly. 'Through the door of your office.'

'Through the glass?'

'Yes.'

'Frosted glass doesn't give you a very good view, does it, Raina?'

'You had your arms around her!'

'I probably did,' he agreed, still in that deadly pleasant voice. 'If it was the day I'm thinking of. I don't remember the exact date, but I can remember putting my arms around Angela once. I *wasn't* kissing her, however.'

'Do you expect me to believe that?'

And Logan looked at her with danger in his eyes and said, still softly but much less pleasantly, 'Yes. Yes, I damn well do!'

Raina made a convulsive movement, and he rapped out, 'You just sit there and listen!'

She stilled, and he slowly straightened as though ready to hold her down if she made any move to escape.

He said, 'Angela is a particularly efficient secretary. On the day in question, I'd been having problems with one of our suppliers of parts, and I wasn't in a very patient mood. Then Angela made a couple of silly mistakes—unlike her, and another time I might have shrugged them off. But one of them would have lost us a few thousand dollars if I hadn't picked up the error in time, and I overreacted, I guess. I blew the poor girl up, and—again unexpectedly for her—she burst into tears and started to run out of my office. Well, not being an absolute brute, I went after her, apologised and patted her shoulder by way of showing my contrition. It was something of a surprise when she suddenly turned to me and began sobbing on my shoulder. Not being male, perhaps you won't understand why I put my arms around her—but maybe you *will* understand how a woman who has lost her lover will turn to any sympathetic man for comfort.'

'Comfort?'

'That's all she asked for, Raina. And all I gave her. A few minutes of sympathy while she poured out her troubles. And I won't apologise for that. It was little enough.'

'And paying for her house?' asked Raina. 'Was that part of the comforting process?'

Logan straightened, thrust his hands into his pockets, and said curtly, 'Who told you that?'

'No one told me. I heard you talking to Angela, the night of her party.'

'If you were listening——'

'I wasn't *listening*! Not deliberately. I went outside for some air, and you were talking . . .'

'Then you must know part of the story. I suppose you'd better hear it all. Angela had been living with a man for several years. She assumed that one day they'd marry. They pooled their resources like a married couple, and she never bothered to check that the various things she helped to pay for were in both their names. She didn't think it mattered. For a girl who's so on the ball in business, she was incredibly silly in her private life. Well, the boy-friend found a new lady, and when Angela found out about it he reminded her that the flat they shared was his, and if she didn't like what he was doing, she could leave.'

'And she left?'

'She left. Without a thing to show for several years of building up a home, and with very little money. She couldn't believe it when he haggled over what he claimed was his property, and she didn't have the heart to fight over it. She'd given him money, too—straight cash that he was supposed to have invested. She has no receipts and he swore he would never admit to having had it. She was homeless and practically penniless, and thoroughly miserable. She was living in a hostel and trying to piece her life together, and I bawled her out for a petty mistake and precipitated a crisis. The money for the town house, by the way, is a loan. I felt I could at least do that for the poor kid.'

'The ex-boy-friend you referred to,' said Raina, 'was *he* the one she invited to the party?'

'Yes. It's enough to make one think it's true that brains and beauty don't go together. Except that in other areas her brain is exceptionally keen. He spun her a tale about wanting her back, and tried to make her believe that he'd only refused to give up her money and the rest because he wanted to force her to return to him—because he loved her! She said she only invited him out of a sort of bravado—to show him she could do without him—but I suspect that she was tempted to believe him. He turned a bit nasty at the party, though, and I think that cooked his goose. I certainly hope so. She's too nice a girl to throw herself away on a complete bastard like that.'

'You—admire Angela a lot, don't you?' said Raina.

'Yes. I also think she's a fool. I'm not in love with her.'

Raina said in a small voice, 'Could I have my drink back now?'

Logan handed it to her and said, '*Did* you think I was in love with Angela?'.

'I thought—she was your mistress.'

There was a lengthy silence. Then Logan said, 'Thanks!'

'I'm sorry. You don't know how that conversation sounded, from my point of view.'

'Your point of view is pretty biased, isn't it?' he asked bitingly. 'You would put the worst possible construction on anything I said.'

'That's unfair!' she protested.

'Yes,' he agreed, 'I suppose it is. I don't have any edge on you in being unfair, though, do I?'

'I've already apologised, Logan.'

'So don't rub it in? All right, I promise not to bring it up again.'

He took his own glass from the mantelpiece and went over to the window. He stood with his back to her, staring out between the curtains. Raina didn't know what he was looking at, because it was dark outside, now.

She finished her sherry and stood up and, holding her empty glass in both hands, said, 'Logan?'

He glanced over his shoulder, and said curtly, 'Yes?'

'You said that you loved *me*. Do you—still?'

He stood perfectly still, she could see only his back. And when he turned at last to face her, his face was the hard mocking mask she hated.

'You ask for a lot, don't you?' he drawled.

'I don't know what you mean.'

'What do you want? A confession of undying love? Sorry, Raina, I can't oblige.'

She had never believed the hurt could be so great. She stood rock-still on the carpet, her hands clutching the glass between them, and she felt as if the whole world had just fallen away and left her standing on some horrible precipice where one step would bring destruction.

White to the lips, she said, 'Can't? Or—won't?' Because this was something she had to know. And if she had to bear the answer she dreaded, she would, somehow . . .

'Clever little lady!' Logan said disagreeably. He half turned and put his glass down on the nearest windowsill, his face stark and angry. 'I'm not in the mood for this conversation,' he said, beginning to walk towards the door. 'A man can take just so much of this!'

'Of what?' Raina cried.

He stopped just before he got to the doorway, and looked back at her. 'This one-sided loving,' he said. 'Maybe I'm selfish,' he continued. 'God knows I ran out of patience long since. Perhaps I don't love you enough, though what I feel for you tears me apart every time I look at you—I should be able to forgive you, I suppose, for not trusting me. Well, I don't feel forgiving—I feel savage about it. I feel savage about a lot of things—including your desire to probe my emotions, all of a sudden. *Why?* Is it just to feed your vanity? Or are you afraid of the meal ticket you married me for, disappearing? You needn't worry, you know. I'll never willingly let you go. Not after all these years of wanting you. You're my life—you're in my head and in my heart and in the air that I breathe. Every conscious moment is filled with you, and I wake every day with your name singing in my mind. I hunger for you every night, and I lie there in that spare bed, sick with longing for you, and sweating because if I come to you, it will be a rape.

'There have even been times when I've *wanted* that— to take you with violence, to show as little consideration for your feelings as you have for mine, to punish you for what you've brought me to,' he admitted. 'Sometimes I'd think about that, and it would seem like a damned good idea. And then I'd think about what might happen afterwards—would you look at me even more coldly than you do? Supposing you cringed from me? Could I stand it if I made you afraid of me? And what if you left me? And do you know what? It was that thought that stopped me every time—because if it's a daily torment having you in my life and in my home, watching you every day and listening to your voice, being a father to your son, the thought of your *not* being here fills me with terror.

'Yes , I love you, Raina. Why should I deny you the satisfaction of hearing me say it? I've given you everything but the last tattered remnants of my pride. Why hang on to that? What's it worth, anyway, if I don't have you?'

His voice was bitter. *'I love you, I love you, I love you,'* he said. 'Is that what you want to hear? I don't give a damn that you don't love me, though once I was fool enough to think that you—wanted me, at least. Maybe I just needed to think so, maybe my own feelings for you blinded me to what you really felt—or didn't feel. I don't know any more. I don't care. All I care about is having you near me, where I can breathe the same air you breathe, eat at the same table, live in the same house, care about the same child. Because the hell of having you near me, and knowing you don't want me, is infinitely preferable to the hell of not having you at all.'

Raina stood staring at the starkness of his face, the bitterness in his eyes, an invisible trembling within her. She heard his harsh breathing, and she herself didn't seem to be breathing at all. She felt unsafe, in spite of the solid floor beneath her feet. She felt she couldn't, didn't dare, to move.

Logan drew in a shuddering breath, and his shoulders dropped a little, as though he was suddenly tired. 'Well,' he said, his voice quiet, with a faint shadow of mockery returning to it, 'now you know.'

When he moved, turning again towards the door, Raina moved, too, almost blindly going to the mantelpiece and fumbling as she put down her glass on it. Her fingers ached from holding it so tightly, and her throat felt raw.

She couldn't look at Logan, but she knew he was going out, and that she had to stop him. Quite clearly, still facing the fireplace and holding on to the mantel to steady herself, because she needed that, she said, 'I want you, Logan. I always have.'

CHAPTER NINE

FOR a moment the silence was total. Then she sensed that Logan had turned, was coming towards her, very slowly. She released her grip on the mantel, and the trembling of her body couldn't be contained any longer. She put shaking hands to her mouth as Logan said, close behind her, 'Say that again, Raina.'

'I—want you,' she whispered shakenly. 'I've wanted you since the first time you kissed me.'

There was a long pause, then he said, his voice not quite steady, 'That's quite an admission.'

His hands turned her quite gently, until she was in his arms, held so closely that the trembling stopped. His eyes searched her face, and he said, 'It's enough. It's enough—for now.'

His kiss bruised, but she met it with her arms about his neck, her mouth responsive, her passion a match for his. And after a long while his mouth became more gentle, though there was still a latent violence in the way he held her. He tugged back her head with his fingers in her hair, and down the curve of her throat he drew a line of scorching kisses, making her gasp with pleasure. A low laugh sounded deep in his throat, and his hands on her hips pushed her almost roughly even closer to him, making her fully aware of his desire. She muffled a cry against his shirt, but one of his hands went to her chin and forced it up, and he watched with merciless eyes the flaming colour in her cheeks, the answering desire in her eyes, before his lips once more parted hers.

Her desire was a vortex, a spinning, dark, ever-quickening tide, and its centre was Logan, Logan's hands, his mouth, his body—his love.

He lifted his mouth at last from hers and she said in a soft, urgent whisper, 'Love me, Logan. Please—please love me.'

'Yes,' he said. 'Yes.'

Raina clung to him as he carried her to the bedroom, their mouths still finding each other, breaking apart and then almost desperately coming together again, her arms tight about his neck and his holding her so closely that the softness of her breasts was crushed against him, but she didn't mind.

He placed her gently on the bed, and she lay still, her arms open at her sides, ready to welcome him, and watched unashamedly as he shrugged off his clothes in the dimness. When he had finished, she moved her hand towards him, but instead of lying beside her he knelt by the bed, taking her hand in his, kissing her palm and then her wrist. Then he leaned over and kissed her mouth briefly, his lips softer and gentle, the violence contained and controlled. He pressed another gentle kiss on her throat, then raised his head and slowly began undoing the buttons on her blouse, leaving a line of kisses in their place as he pulled them open.

By the time he had undressed her completely, her whole body knew the intimate touch of his mouth, and she was on fire with her love for him. When at last he joined her on the bed, his lean male body beautifully fitted to her soft woman's contours, she was ready to give him anything he wanted, anything he demanded of her.

In the darkness, he said, 'Tell me you love me. I don't care if it isn't true. Say it.'

Raina said it, over and over, whispered it in his ear, cried it out to the darkness as their loving reached its overwhelming culmination, murmured it against his throat moments later before she slipped into sleep. She knew he wanted to hear her say it, and that it excited him beyond measure, and his excitement fed hers. It was like an incantation, or a love potion, as potent in its effect as some ancient aphrodisiacal spell. It had the power to make him tremble, and it was a sweet power, and heady.

She woke with a delicious, languorous feeling of well-being, and opened her eyes to find Logan propped on his elbow beside her, watching her.

She said, 'Logan.'

'Yes?' His voice was deep and quiet, his eyes on her flushed face alight with a kind of sensuous satisfaction.

'Nothing,' she said. Her hand moved towards him, and he took it in strong, warm fingers, and bent his head to put his lips to her wrist as he had the night before, his mouth open, his tongue running along the narrow blue vein. Her fingers curled and then opened, and her eyes half closed with pleasure, her lips slightly parted.

Logan lifted his mouth, and it was firm and unsmiling, but his eyes smiled, and hers returned it. He still held her hand, and the index finger of his other hand ran softly along her inner arm to the crook of her elbow, and his dark head went down to plant another kiss there.

Raina heard sounds in the bathroom and said, 'Danny's up.'

Logan reluctantly lifted his head and said, 'The little monster. Doesn't he know it's Sunday?'

'Oh, I see,' she said. 'Now that you've had your wicked way with me, my son's just a little monster.'

He grinned, very full of himself. 'Sure,' he said. 'Since you've discovered my evil designs, I'll set him among the cinders—is he big enough to make us breakfast in bed?'

'No. Not without supervision, anyway. Is that what you want?'

He gave her a long, significant look. 'No, but I'd settle for it as a substitute.'

Raina made a face at him, her eyes smiling. 'I always knew you were a man of brutish passions!'

'Mmm,' he said and, making a low growling noise in his throat, reached for her as she gave a laughing little scream and tried to lunge away.

Danny came in and saw them both laughing as she struggled in Logan's grasp. He erupted on to the bed and gleefully joined in, seizing a pillow and attacking Logan with it, until Logan pretended he was beaten and let Raina go. They lay back, panting and smiling, and Danny wriggled into the bed between them and said, 'What are we going to do today?'

Logan gave a mock groan, and Raina laughed and said, 'Let's go to church, for a start.'

'Why?' Danny asked.

And Logan said, 'To give thanks.'

His eyes met Raina's across Danny's head, and she saw a question in his that she couldn't read.

'Yes,' she said. 'To give thanks.'

It seemed to satisfy him.

But in the days and weeks that followed, Raina was to see that questioning look again. Their days were filled with laughter and their nights with passion, and Danny was thriving in an atmosphere where the undercurrents of tension no longer existed. And yet there was still in Logan a faint watchfulness, an air of waiting.

But if she raised her brows in a query, his mouth would curve into a smile, making the look disappear, so that she thought she had imagined it. And if she asked, when they were alone, 'What is it? What's the matter?' he would say, 'What could be the matter?' and before she could remark on the sardonic note in his voice, he would say, 'Come here, kiss me, I want you.' And the moment would be lost in the drowning sweetness of his lovemaking.

The play-centre was holding a Fathers' Day on a Saturday morning to give the men a chance to spend some time with their children and to involve them in the centre's activities. Raina couldn't understand Danny's indifference to the idea, until he said, 'I haven't got a father to come. My Daddy can't come, can he?'

'Uncle Logan will come instead,' she said gently. 'That's just the same as having your daddy there.'

He looked doubtful, and she said, 'Some of the other boys and girls don't have their daddies, either, you know. Shona's going to bring her granddad, instead.'

'How do you know?'

'Shona's mother told me,' Raina smiled. Shona's mother was a solo mother who lived with her parents, and counted herself very lucky in their help to bring up her daughter.

'I wish my daddy could come,' Danny muttered. '*And* Uncle Logan.'

'Well, I'm sure Uncle Logan will,' Raina promised.

She didn't tell Logan about the conversation, though it troubled her. Perhaps she should encourage Danny to give Logan the name *Daddy*. She hadn't thought it mattered what title he had, and *Uncle* was what Danny was used to, and as good as any. But was he going to feel deprived of a 'real' father? His memory of Perry must be extremely hazy, even now. She wondered if he really remembered his father, at all.

Logan came, and Raina watched him with a hint of amusement mingled with surprise as he talked and worked with not only Danny, but some of the other children as well. She would have said Logan was unlikely father material, although he had always been good with Danny. But he showed no awkwardness, his manner casual and uncondescending as it had always been with Danny, and the children responded with trusting friendliness.

The women tended to sit back and watch as the children dragged the men about to show them the painting easels, the puzzles, the dressing-up corner, and all the delights of the centre, and demanded to be helped with ambitious projects at the carpentry bench, or in the sandpit. Logan got cornered into reading a fairy tale to Danny and a few others, while a little girl leaned against his knee to look at the pictures. Raina watched from a few yards away, her eyes alight with laughter as Logan solemnly intoned, 'And they all lived happily ever after!' closing the book with palpable relief, and immediately standing up to signify he felt his duty in that direction was done.

He caught her eye and, coming over to her, nipped her arm in retribution, saying under his breath, 'You may laugh! You've loved getting me into this, haven't you?'

'You're enjoying it!' she said. 'Admit it.'

'I admit nothing. They corrected every mistake I made, and wouldn't let me skip a word. If they know the dratted book off by heart, why ask me to read it to them?'

Danny pulled at Logan's arm. 'Come and push me on the *big* swing!' he demanded, adding graciously, 'You can watch, Mummy!'

Knowing full well that Danny had long since mastered the art of 'pushing' himself, Raina stood meekly by and watched Logan send Danny higher and higher, as he demanded, in the tire swing attached to the high branch ot a puriri tree.

'That's enough! That's enough!' Danny cried at last, and Logan, pretending exhaustion, leaned on the trunk of the tree next to Raina.

Danny was leaning back in the swing, his eyes closed, as it swung lower and slower. 'You're a good pusher, Uncle Logan,' he said dreamily.

'Thank you,' Logan said gravely.

'Will you always be my Uncle Logan?'

'If you want me to be.'

'Are you Mummy's daddy?'

'No, I'm Mummy's husband.'

'You mean you married my mummy.'

'That's right. You were there, remember?'

'Well, Simon's mummy got married, and that man's Simon's new daddy, because his other daddy went away.'

Logan straightened suddenly, and said, his voice carefully casual, 'Did he? Is Simon's new daddy here today?'

'Yes. He's nice.'

Logan's eyes were on Danny, his soft brown head resting against the rope of the swing now, as it rocked gently back and forth, his legs dangling so that his dusty sneakers almost touched the worn ground, dark lashes hiding his eyes. Logan's hand went out suddenly and closed on Raina's arm, and he said, still looking only at the child, 'Marrying your mother entitles me to be *your* new daddy, if you'd like that. You can call me Daddy if you want to, you know.'

'Can I?' The swing twisted a little as Danny wriggled, but he didn't look up. 'Okay,' he said, as though conceding a favour, and his toe touched the ground, stopping the swing's movement. He slithered to the ground and looked about, and suddenly darted off to the small trampoline, where his friend Shaun was performing acrobatically for his parents.

Raina's eyes were shimmering with tears, and Logan shifted to stand in front of her, shielding her from the view of anyone who might be looking. *'Don't!'* he said roughly. She went to raise her fingers to brush away the tears, but his were there first, much more gentle than his voice. 'He can scarcely remember his father,' he said harshly. 'What would you expect?'

She caught his wrist and said, 'It's all right. I'm sorry, I didn't mean to cry.'

He made a sharp, exasperated sound under his breath, and she said quickly, 'You haven't met Sally's husband, have you—Shaun's father? I'll introduce you.'

Logan gave her a searching, frowning look and she met it with a glancing smile and moved away so that he had to follow her over to where the Frenches were standing, and be introduced to Bill, whose placid normality was a guaranteed antidote to any fraughtness that happened to be about.

That night his lovemaking was tinged with violence, so that while Raina revelled in his passion, she was almost frightened by the ways in which he expressed it. When it had spent itself, she ran her tongue over throbbing lips, and touched a fingertip to them. Logan lay on his back, no longer touching her, staring into the darkness, but he turned his head at her movement and asked, 'What is it? Was I rough?'

'A bit,' she said, trying to smile.

He looked at her rather broodingly and said, 'I'm sorry. I didn't mean to hurt you.'

He got up abruptly and shrugged into a dark robe and went over to the window, pushing aside the curtain to stare down at the distant gleam of the river.

'You cried, today,' he said. 'Why did you cry?'

'I—don't know, really.'

He turned his head sharply and said, 'Let's agree to be honest with each other, Raina. A marriage can't live on lies.'

'I'm not lying,' she said. 'It was—an emotional moment, that's all. I can't really explain——'

'Try.'

'Is it important?'

'It's very important to me.'

'Well, I was a little sad, I think—for Danny's sake, because he loved Perry and he missed him a lot, at first. But mostly I think I was crying because I know it's bothered him, not having a father of his own, and I was happy that—he'd decided to accept you as his daddy.'

There was a long silence, and Logan hadn't moved. Then he said, in an odd voice, 'And that's the truth?'

'It's as near as I can put it into words.'

He gave an odd, breathy little laugh. 'I thought it was something quite different,' he confessed. 'It's odd—I was never jealous of Perry when he was alive.'

He stopped there, almost as though he would have gone on, but had changed his mind.

Raina watched his shadowy figure in the darkness,

and said, 'You have no need to be jealous of him now, Logan.'

He didn't answer, and she suddenly knew what the strange questioning in his eyes meant. She couldn't see it, now. But she knew that it was there. 'You have no need,' she repeated.

'Tell me *now*!' he said, with sudden urgency, and she caught her breath, understanding what he meant. 'I love you,' she said steadily. 'In cold blood, Logan, without the heat of passion to make me say it. I love you in daylight and darkness, in tenderness and in anger, every day of my life. I love you.'

She got out of the bed and went to him, her bare feet padding over the carpet, moonlight shimmering through the flimsy nightgown she wore.

Logan said, 'How long?'

She knew he didn't mean, *how long will you love me?* but, *how long have you loved me?*

Facing him, she said, 'I don't know when it became love, Logan. Do you?'

'I know,' he said, speaking of himself. 'Do you remember a day when you tripped on the steps outside the office? That's when I knew that I loved you. Before that, I'd thought you were playing me on a string— enjoying it. I thought you knew exactly what it was all about, that probably I wasn't the only one ... I thought—that if I ever did make a pass, you'd probably pretend to be insulted, but you'd secretly get a kick out of it. On those terms, I didn't find the temptation all that difficult to resist. Even when you stumbled, that day, for a moment I wondered if you'd planned it.'

Raina gasped, and he shifted a little, dug his hands into the pockets of his robe. 'All right,' he said, 'I'm a conceited swine—I can't deny that—I'll admit freely you never gave me the least encouragement. But there were sparks between us, Raina. I wasn't so blind or so in-experienced that I didn't know what they meant, and that the kind of sexual antagonism that existed between us couldn't be attributed solely to *my* feelings. It wasn't until I saw how frightened you were, and how totally shocked, that it dawned on me that none of it was de-liberate, that you were fighting it just as hard as I was, in your own way.'

'I wouldn't even admit it to myself,' she said quietly. 'I couldn't—I didn't even know what it was, until that day. And then I simply refused to believe it. I loved Perry—how could I admit I was attracted to another man?'

'I know. The fact is, if I'd seen you first, it would have been me that you married.'

She knew the truth of that, and admitted it at last. 'Yes,' she said. 'But, Logan, I'm glad we kept it from Perry. He kept your friendship—and my love—until the end. If he had ever guessed how we felt——'

And Logan said, 'Perry knew.'

It hit her like a shock wave, made more devastating by the quiet certainty in Logan's voice. Her mind rejected it, her voice wavered high as she protested, *'No! No, he couldn't have—there was nothing——!'*

'There was nothing to be ashamed of!' said Logan. He took a ragged breath. 'You've got to look at it honestly, Raina. If you don't, those guilt feelings of yours are going to haunt our marriage for ever. You don't need to feel guilty about anything, darling. You loved Perry and were loyal to him, in every way. There is no shame in attracting another man's love—there's no sin in being attracted. And that's all it was, an at-traction which you denied even to yourself, as you've just told me. So vehemently that you kept on denying it long after he was dead, with a misguided gallantry that made me so angry with you I wanted to beat you, and so proud of you that I could have wept. There was a certain irony in that, because if I loved you first for anything, it was for your loyalty to Perry.'

'But—if he knew——'

'He knew,' Logan repeated. 'And he—enjoyed it.' He waited while that sank in, then said slowly, 'I've realised, long since, that there are things about Perry I've always known, which you never discovered. A man shows different faces to his wife and to his best friend, I suppose. Or perhaps it's just that I knew him when we were both too young to be able to hide much. There was nothing malicious in Perry, but there was a certain amount of—envy, I suppose you'd call it, for want of a better word. You said once that he hero-worshipped me. He didn't. He wanted to be like me. Lord knows why—he was a pretty brilliant sort of person himself. But because of his envy, he always particularly liked it if he could be one up on me. It didn't hurt me—usually. It was part of his personality. Maybe not the most attractive part, but who's perfect? I didn't mind. He had a lot of very attractive qualities that made up for it. Many more than I have.'

There were a number of things Raina could have replied to that, but he wasn't fishing, and she didn't speak.

'It might help you to understand,' Logan went on, 'if I tell you about an incident that's stuck in my mind, from way back. The home where we were brought up didn't have a great deal in the way of toys. What there was mostly had to be shared. But at Christmas they made sure everyone got something for themselves. Perry and I were pretty close, as you know. Mostly, we shared everything. But one Christmas he got a fire-engine, and for some reason I took a particular fancy to it. I offered to swop it for the police car that _I_ had got. Perry wouldn't do it. Well, that was his privilege. But the fire-engine was the one thing he would never let me play with. He kept taking it out in front of me, and he'd say, "Look, Logan, isn't it a beauty," without any thought of malice—he just wanted to show it off, and I think he genuinely thought watching him play with it was the next best thing to playing with it myself. But he would never let me touch it.'

He paused again, and Raina stood motionless, waiting for him to go on.

'When I realised how I felt about you,' said Logan, 'I was ready to somehow get out—go away. I started the Australian connection with the thought in mind that I could go there, make it an excuse to leave. Perry wouldn't have it. Your name never came up, but it was quite plain. Perry didn't want to lose either of us. That was one thing. He trusted us both—that was another. But the crux of the matter was that he realised he had the woman I wanted, and—he liked that, Raina. He liked it very much. Maybe I should have cut and run, anyway. But I didn't. I stayed, and Perry, at least, was happy.'

Raina shivered. 'You said, once, he knew us both very well,' she said. 'This—was what you meant?'

'Yes.'

'He knew how I felt?'

'I'm pretty sure he did. He also knew that you would never let him down. That he was always first with you.'

'But he was unfaithful to me.'

Logan moved sharply. 'I told you, that was a lie.'

'Oh, no!' she said. 'I know which was the lie.'

'I should never have said it,' he admitted harshly.

'But you did. And it *was* true, wasn't it? He thought you were something of a Don Juan, you know. Was he emulating you in that, too?'

'Possibly. I'm not the rake he liked to imagine,

actually. Anyway, it wasn't anything for you to be concerned about. Just a casual encounter that I happened to find out about. I never came nearer to hitting Perry in my life.'

'There might have been others.'

He didn't deny that. 'It was nothing more than a stupid prank,' he said. 'He loved you, no one else.'

'It doesn't hurt now,' said Raina. 'I expect he didn't intend anything to come of it, and then when it was too late to back out, he thought it wasn't important enough to matter, if I never knew.'

'Perhaps you knew him better than I thought.'

'Perhaps. He *was* like that, wasn't he?'

'Yes, he was like that.'

There was a silence, the night enwrapping them with a soft melancholy, and she said, 'Logan, he would have liked it, wouldn't he—that you and I got married?'

She knew she was pleading for a reassurance, for, perhaps, a justification. And as the words left her lips, she had the sudden conviction that it was not going to be given.

Logan's reply was so long in coming that she thought he was leaving it like that, in the air. But then he said with brutal deliberation, 'I think that Perry would have destroyed that fire-engine, rather than let me have it— ever.'

Raina closed her eyes, trembling, for long moments almost hating him for doing this to her. But she knew why he did it. The truth was necessary between them, so that their new loving was not based on illusions, on fantasies, on lies, so that nothing of the long pretence could cast its shadow on their love.

'He asked you to care for us,' she whispered. 'You said so.'

'He did. And I did promise. It was a gesture, Raina. I

don't think that Perry believed, right to the last, that he could really die. And if he did—he thought that you and I would continue to pretend, as though he was still alive. As you did.'

And as Logan had never done.

And if Perry had died believing that his wife and his friend would continue the long self-denial that they had begun for his sake, had they betrayed him, now?

'Oh, God!' she whispered.

Logan was strangely silent, and she knew that he was aware of all her thoughts, that he was waiting, letting her receive the implications, sort them for herself, decide on them.

It took her long minutes, and she was trembling, one hand clutching at the curtain for support, the other clenched against her stomach, because there was something painful and terrifying about her thoughts.

'I told you,' said Logan at last, his voice quiet, almost weary, defeated. 'I told you that I married you for myself, not for Danny, not for Perry.'

'Yes,' she said. 'Yes.'

She turned away from him, and then back again. 'Perry would have hated it,' she said. 'Wouldn't he?'

'Yes,' Logan said uncompromisingly, 'Perry would have hated it.'

Raina let out a long sigh, and her taut figure suddenly relaxed. 'It doesn't matter,' she said clearly. 'It isn't important, any more, how Perry would have felt, not now . . .'

The last string was cut, and she said, 'I loved him, and you know that. But that love is nothing to do with you and me. I married you, Logan, because I wanted to, and I wanted to because, if I didn't love you then, I knew that I would love you, even if I didn't want to admit it. Perry is in the past, and you wouldn't want me to take back what I gave to him. But I love you, Logan. And I want your love more than anything in the world.'

'Oh, God!' he said softly. 'It's been such a long wait, Raina. To hear you say it, and know you mean it, that it isn't just passion, or pretence, or pity.'

She went into his arms, and told him again, without pretence or pity, but with a passion that needed no words.

And he believed.

Harlequin Plus

WHAT'S IN A NAME?

Following is a list of some of the most popular female names in Britain and North America today. We thought you might enjoy knowing the meanings of these names, and the language from which they were derived.

Name	Meaning
Amanda	worthy of love (Latin)
Catherine	the pure (Greek)
Claire	bright and shining (Latin)
Deborah	the bee (Hebrew)
Emma	the healer (Teutonic)
Helen	light (Greek)
Joanne (Jane)	God's gracious gift (Hebrew)
Julie (Julia)	youthful (Greek)
Karen	the pure (Greek)
Kelly	a fountain or spring (Old Norse)
Lisa (Elizabeth)	oath of God (Hebrew)
Louise	battle maiden (Teutonic)
Michelle	who is like God (Hebrew)
Nicola	victory of the people (Greek)
Rachel	ewelike (Hebrew)
Rebecca	to bind (Hebrew)
Samantha	the listener (Aramaic, Semitic language)
Sarah	princess (Hebrew)
Tracy	the brave (Anglo-Saxon)
Victoria	victory (Latin)

By the way, our author's name, Daphne, though not common, has a lovely derivation: it is Greek for "laurel," a leafy tree common to southern Europe and used in ancient Greece to crown the victors in the Pythian games. There are many other names derived from trees or flowers, and among them are those of several more Harlequin authors—Violet, Rosemary, Flora, Ivy and Iris!

The compelling Irish Saga

The Defiant

MARY CANON

For centuries there has been no love lost between the Irish and the English. But for a brief moment in time, at the court of Elizabeth I, a forbidden love was found...between a steel-willed Irish spy and a high-spirited English beauty. Their love created a powerful family, and an even more powerful legend.

1981 BEST SELLER

FROM
WORLDWIDE LIBRARY

Available wherever paperback books are sold.